DARK

BOOK TWO OF THE SCORPION CHRONICLES

RUSSELL TURNBULL

RUSSELL TURNBULL STUDIOS

THE SCORPION CHRONICLES

Hollow: Book One

Dark: Book Two

Vast: Book Three

DEDICATION

I would like to start out by thanking my wife...

Thank you, Tania, for all of your help and support throughout this long process of creating and bringing to life a completely new world of wonderful possibilities and adventure.

Without your help and support, these books would never have been completed.

You have proved repeatedly that with you by my side, anything, yes, anything is possible.

I love you dearly.

You are the best part of my life.

I would also like to thank Ms. Michele Golden for your help and support.

Thanks also to Brian Abbott for the great new character idea!

This book is dedicated to my son Christopher, my wife Tania and all else that helped and supported me in the magical process of Literary World Creation.

CONTENTS

AUTHOR'S NOTES

Welcome back to the Realm of Beornan Heafod for the second installment of The Scorpion Chronicles.

The Prologue that you are about to read is actually intended for those who have NOT read The Scorpion Chronicles: Book One – Hollow. If that's you, I have summed up most of what you will need to know in order to understand what is going on in this, Book Two.

For those of you who are continuing from Book One, you are MORE than welcome to read the Prologue as a refresher, or you can simply skip to the beginning of Chapter One and continue with the story... The choice is completely yours.

You will notice that I have continued to use archaic words that are no longer used in today's language as well as foreign words, but by using your context clues; it should not be difficult to understand their meanings.

I really hope that you enjoy this book as much as you enjoyed Book One.

Thanks...

Russell Turnbull

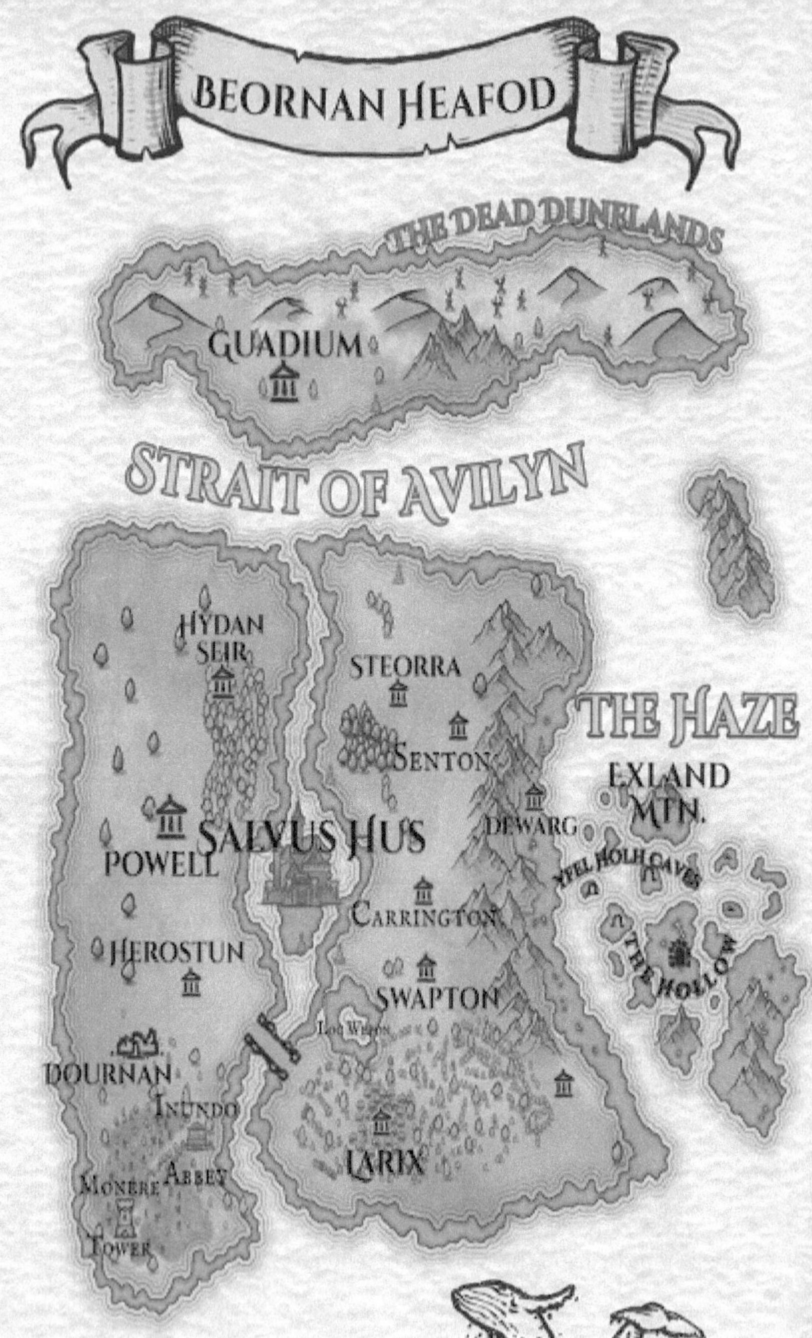

BEORNAN HEAFOD
THE DEAD DUNELANDS
GUADIUM
STRAIT OF AVILYN
HYDAN SEIR
STEORRA
THE HAZE
SENTON
EXLAND MTN.
POWELL
SALVUS HUS
DEWARG
YFEL HOLH CAVES
CARRINGTON
THE HOLLOW
HEROSTUN
SWAPTON
LOD WILTON
DOURNAN
INUNDO
LARIX
MONERE ABBEY
TOWER

PROLOGUE

A FEW DAYS AGO...

A low ground fog was beginning to creep from the lower parts of the land, crawling out over the area like ghostly hands with skeletal fingers.

The constant cry of a distant whippoorwill drowned out the shrill chirps of thousands of crickets looking for their mates.

I quickly jumped down from my horse while Brother Fost and Sir Quinn followed suit.

Brother Fost quickly began to bless each and every bolt that was loaded on his crossbow and I could hear Meeka chanting a spell from somewhere behind us.

The vampire opened its mouth in a menacing, grizzly smile.

Its lips pulled back over its teeth, showing incisors and canines that reminded me of a tomcat I once had as a child; they were sparkling pinkish white and looked to be dagger sharp.

The vampire's smile drew up into haunting eyes that were red rimmed, sunken in and black like the dead eyes of a doll.

"Don't look at its eyes!" The priest called out as a warning, "Do not look it in the eyes!" He repeated and continued to call out to us.

Quickly, I lowered my gaze and noticed a few hundred rats moving about the vampire's feet creating the odd effect of a shadow; the rats pooled around it like some sort of large carpet of flesh and fur.

The wind picked up and carried the nefarious rank stench of carrion.

Clouds moved across the sky, threatening to cover up the sliver of the moon that closely resembled a cat's eye; making it difficult to see in the gathering gloom.

"Shouldn't we have a full moon for an occasion such as this?" I quipped, trying to lessen my own fear.

The vampire's smile widened and it let out a ghoulish laugh; apparently, it, but no one else thought what I had said was funny.

"Let the girl go!" Brother Fost commanded again.

The vampire quickly canceled its smile, hissed, drew the girl back and then violently threw her at the priest, landing her on him with a bone breaking crash; his crossbow was knocked out of reach.

"Be careful what you wish for, holy man!" The vampire gurgled in a voice that was as un-human as the howl of a wolf.

I slowly took a step forward toward the vampire.

The vampire took a step forward toward me.

I stepped to my left, toward the fallen priest.

The vampire stepped to its right. (My left.)

Meeka's chanting had stopped and I could feel a strange sort of tingling sensation on the back of my neck, down through my spine and out through my feet.

Fireflies began to blink everywhere around us, apparently unafraid of the undead creature in their midst.

I could feel the vampire's gaze trying to burn a hole deep into my soul, trying (and failing) to make me look it in its eyes.

I slid to my left a bit more... (Monkey see...)

The vampire slid to its right as well... (Monkey do.)

The tingling in my body began to spread into my arms and then into my hands and fingers.

I felt a sharp shock in my left hand that made me jump a bit.

(Simon says...)

The vampire did nothing. (This was all happening very quickly...)

I decided to take a chance and dive for Brother Fost's Blessed Crossbow, as I could see it from the corner of my eye.

Meeka must have foreseen my every move, because as soon as I dove for the Blessed Crossbow, the vampire quickly moved forward toward me. (Or tried to.)

As soon as the vampire made its move, (when I made **my** move,) Meeka made her move and cast a 'lightning' spell that arced across the expanse and engulfed the vampire, knocking it away from Brother Fost and myself.

I landed in a tuck-and-roll with the Blessed Crossbow firmly in my hand.

The vampire had landed on its back with rats scattering everywhere, they were fleeing, and escaping further danger.

I stood up...

The vampire stood up.

I pulled the crossbow's trigger, launching a Holy Bolt at the undead fiend, which bounced harmlessly off a hidden armor plate under the vampire's clothes, protecting its vital, yet un-beating heart.

The vampire laughed again, bearing sharp jagged teeth that looked nastier this time than they did the last.

Loher let loose an arrow that buried itself into the vampire's right shoulder.

The vampire hissed and yanked the arrow out.

I fired off another Holy Bolt, finding purchase in the vile creature's neck.

Vaporous smoke escaped from the wound.

The vampire shrieked out in pain, but yanked that bolt out as well.

It looked as though the vampire was going to make a sudden move to attack, when unexpectedly, a large mass of the fireflies swarmed around its face. (Fireflies?)

Balt and Sir Quinn took this chance to rescue Brother Fost and the unconscious girl and drag them off into the safety within the walls of Powell.

Meeka began to round up our mounts.

I quickly realized that the fireflies were not fireflies at all, but fairies and the sprite, Brendt!

More and more of the tiny glowing creatures arrived in full force and surrounded the vampire engulfing its entire body, slowly at first, but then as they became a larger group, they became stronger and stronger.

The vampire howled in anger and confusion, cursing violently as it began to try to escape by changing into a vapor cloud.

"I'll make you **pay**... with your **soul**, Ranger!!" The vampire promised as it escaped, mixing into the fog and mist, vaporizing away.

(THE NEXT DAY...)

I have not been everywhere within the Realm of Beornan Heafod, but I am quite sure we were no longer in Beornan Heafod, or anywhere near it anymore.

There was something strange about the way it felt there outside the strange brick dwelling that housed the witch's coven of the Circle of Flowers; even the air smelled and tasted different.

Odd, low, powerful noises rumbled from unseen places and it was probably a good thing that we were ushered into the brick dwelling so quickly, because I thought I saw a silverish-grey dragon soaring with spread wings, high, so very high in the sky overhead.

We were being led by a human woman wearing strange, almost tight fitting robes.

She led us through a door and then directly down a flight of wooden stairs and into a dark passage.

My night vision picked up on the cold shapes of oddly shaped crates on shelves.

We were then led through another door and into a large room that was brightly lit, which was quite the opposite of what I had always expected the meeting place for a coven of witches would be like. (In my own mind.)

The light was emanating from small glass pear-shaped globes, which were covered by cylindrical shades that were narrow at the top and wide at the bottom.

The globes and shades were on wooden stands attached to the wall by long, slim, leash-like contraptions.

The witch's altar was set up in the middle of the room on a large, long rectangular table that was covered in tight green felt.

There were netted holes in each corner of the table, as well as in the center of both long sides, almost as if they were meant to catch something.

At one end of the altar sat a number of solid-colored and striped orbs about the size of an apple, while a pair of slender poles – almost like thin jousting sticks – rested against the altar next to the orbs.

The remainder of the altar was set as I had always imagined a witch's altar would look like, with colored candles, various bowls which held sands and herbs and other unidentifiable reagents, crystal goblets, athames (sacred knives,) stones, tomes, and perhaps a skull or two.

There was even an assortment of large feathers that ranged in colors from black through grey to speckled white.

Strange, enchanting music floated everywhere about the room from an unknown source.

Affixed upon the wall, very near the business end of the altar hung the holy symbol of witches, a five-pointed star in a circle; the top point was pointing up, making this recognizable as a pentacle.

A half dozen (or more) human men and women stood in a loose group as we were led into the room; the coven members were all wearing strange, slightly similar, almost constricting and very uncomfortable looking clothing.

My companions and I were led to sit in some rather comfortable throne like chairs as the High Priestess began to speak; the others sat and stood, wide eyed gawking at us, quite like the townsfolk in Powell.

"We, of the coven 'The Circle of Flowers' have been trying to keep a close eye on you," the High Priestess began as she walked toward us from the other side of the altar.

"Why us?" I asked, as if coming out of a trance.

The High Priestess smiled and stated, "You have been seen in some of my own clairvoyant visions."

Meeka excitedly spoke up, "Isn't that when you can see the future in a dreamlike state?"

"Correct," the High Priestess answered, still smiling.

"What happens to us in your visions?" Loher demanded.

Suddenly, the High Priestess got a worried look upon her face.

"You might as well tell them, Shannon," a male witch said in a matter-of-a-fact tone, "you **did** bring them here."

The High Priestess, Shannon, shot him an unappreciative look and then reluctantly agreed, "You're right, Jason," she then turned to face us once again, "In my visions, I see one of you turned into a vampire, so I sent my fairies out to protect you."

"That would have been me," I said with an uncomfortable chuckle, "your fairies performed their assignment very well." I complimented.

Shannon and Jason looked at each other with pride in their eyes.

"Pray tell, what would have happened if your fairies had failed?" Loher asked.

"And I had been turned into a vampire?" I finished the question with a shudder.

A grim look washed over the High Priestess' face, "My fairies would have attempted to capture you and bring you to that room," she stated and pointed to a door off to the far side of the room behind us.

"What be in there?" Balt growled before I could ask.

"That room holds an airtight, glass chamber which is escape-proof for vampires." Jason offered.

"We have discovered a way to give a willing vampire back its soul." Shannon answered.

"What do you mean, 'willing'?" I asked.

"The vampire must **want** to regain its soul." Shannon answered.

"If I were a vampire, I would most certainly want my soul returned to my body." I said with complete conviction.

I could not imagine myself being a vampire; soulless, undead.

"Well," Jason declared, "that threat has been stopped; the fairies were successful and you don't have to worry about that anymore." He laughed.

"Indeed." Shannon agreed, "We shall now return you to your own..." Her voice trailed off as if in deep thought.

(Your own... time?)

(LATER...AT THE CASTLE...)

The vampire sequence scared the young King a bit, especially because the vampire is reported as 'At Large' which compelled His Majesty to inform us that he was going to hire a professional vampire hunter at once... Moreover, he did; he called in a messenger and ordered it to be done...

CHAPTER ONE

REFLECTIONS

T ONIGHT...

"I would like to propose a toast!" I announced as I raised my cup, high above the table.

Brendt quickly filled his amethyst cup as well; the whole team joined in by raising their cups and mugs.

"To us and to the triumphant success of a mission completed and in good time!"

"Here here!" My companions replied in agreement.

"Cheers!" We all sang and took long pulls from our drinks... Together... As ONE.

The celebration continued in the 'Broken Blade' as the unrelenting dark clouds rolled in, bringing an unnatural mist along with them.

The townsfolk of Salvus Hus quickly secured their homes for fear of a giant storm.

"Now te perpose a toast Meself," Balt announced as he climbed up to stand on the surface of the table, knocking empty cups and mugs, noisily to the floor; we all began laughing as the dwarf successfully accomplished this feat, "Te ta cap'n an' crew o' Ta Scorpion! Wit'out them, we'd prolly **still** be walkin'!"

A cheer rose up from our table and we all started to applaud our fortunes, but as our applause died down, clapping from the tavern door continued...

My heart raced as I looked at the door, there, clapping, stood the vampire from the outskirts of Powell.

"I'm here to collect your debt, Ranger." The vampire growled in its inhuman, wolf-like voice.

⚬

"Please, allow me to properly introduce myself," the vampire spoke as it strode so swiftly past us to the fire that we had temporarily lost sight of it, "My name is Sawol. Losian Sawol."

"Tat's a mighty foine trick ye got der, Blood Sucker." Balt sneered, still standing on the table.

The vampire just looked back at the dwarf and smiled, revealing rows of dagger like teeth.

A hush suddenly fell like snow upon the tavern.

Patrons of the 'Broken Blade' began slowly edging from their tables toward the door.

Lance, the tavern owner, unexpectedly, from behind the bar, fired off a crossbow bolt at the undead fiend, but once again, the bolt harmlessly bounced off of the vampire's hidden chest plate and lodged itself into the ceiling, just above the vampire's head.

In a flash, the vampire sprung away from the fire and appeared at the bar, holding Lance up by the throat.

Lance was already dead by the time our eyes could focus on the movement, hanging there limply in the vampire's clutches, dripping blood from a gaping wound on his neck.

"Well, let **me** introduce **myself**," a female voice called, from again, the tavern door, "My name is Death. **True death**, for you, Losian!"

Standing there in the doorway, stood a young human woman, about the age of fifteen or sixteen.

She was wearing studded leather armor over full chainmail; her long amber hair fell loosely over her shoulders making her look almost angelic.

In one hand, she held a large wooden case and in the other, a large leather pouch.

She dropped the wooden case where she stood and took a step toward Losian.

The vampire dropped the dead tavern owner and took a step toward the girl.

The girl slowly opened the pouch and widened its top to loosen up its contents.

The vampire only smiled.

In one fluid motion, the girl grabbed the pouch by its bottom and projected its contents at the vampire; a few dozen sharp tipped silver jacks soared through the air and buried themselves into the bar and the wall behind it.

Losian had seen this move coming and had already moved back to the fire, snatching me up on its way.

Before Loher or anyone else in my party could react, it bit into my neck and began to drain me of my life's blood, whispering in my ear, " I **told you** you'd pay with your soul... **Ranger.**"

"Rise away from him you unholy terror!" The girl cried, holding up an ancient holy symbol.

The vampire dropped me as it rose up to its full stature and slowly turned around.

I grasped at my wound with both hands and tried to stop the ebbing flow as blood pooled around me, oozing through my fingers and running down my arms.

Oddly enough, I felt very little to no pain, but the amount of my own blood pouring down to the floor was enough to make me panic, in turn making my heart beat harder and my blood drain faster.

Brother Fost fired off a shot from his Blessed Crossbow, finding purchase in Losian's forehead.

Losian's eyes went wide as it reached for the bolt, while gaseous vapors poured out from the wound; the vampire's skull began to crack and its skin began to blister and peel.

It began to howl and shriek in pain and agony as tiny bright orange flames began to lick out of its wound.

Black smoke could be seen wafting about its head as the tiny flames grew larger, engulfing its face and burning its hair.

The sounds and smells were almost too much to endure as the temperature of the area around the ghastly spectacle began to rapidly rise.

A hideous shriek erupted from the vampire's throat as its head burst into flames.

It was bumping into tables and chairs, setting them ablaze, as the flames descended and quickly consumed the vampire's entire body.

The only things left smoldering on the floor were a pile of ash and the chest plate, melted into an oblong puddle of semi liquid metal.

The tavern emptied out quickly as the remaining patrons all jumped up to their feet, horrified and desperate to escape the rapidly growing blaze.

Brother Fost had finally vanquished the vampire.

Meeka swiftly began putting out the fires with a smaller version of her 'water cone' spell as Loher and Brother Fost quickly ran to my side.

Balt and Sir Quinn began to help patrons to the exit, stamping out small fires as they went.

"Try to heal him Fost!" Loher pleaded.

"Don't touch the ashes!" The girl called in panic as she retrieved her wooden case.

"Who **are** you?" Sir Quinn inquired as the girl inspected the ash.

"My name is Angelique DeStruere," she answered, "I was hired by your King to hunt and vanquish this vampire."

"It looks like our priest did your job for you." Sir Quinn snapped as he inspected the body of the dead tavern owner.

"Don't touch that body either! It has to be destroyed as well." Angelique warned as she scooped and contained the vampire's ashes into a jar and then headed back to her wooden box.

"This **man** is my **friend**!" Sir Quinn argued.

"That **corpse** may turn undead and return to **attack** you...**friend**." The huntress snapped back.

"An' wot about our bitten Mate layin' on ta floor there, **Lassie**?" Balt challenged as he stood between the huntress and me, puffing out his chest.

"Will he have to be killed too?" Kuchoff asked, trying to sound meek.

The huntress looked directly at him with a straight face and calmly answered, "As a matter of a fact, he will."

"**You heartless bitch!**" Loher growled and grabbed the hilt of her sword, "If you come anywhere **near** him, I'll **kill you** myself!"

"He is healed!" Brother Fost exclaimed, relieving some of the tension, "All is well now, I have healed him!"

"IMOPSSIBLE!" The huntress gasped, eyes wide, she took a step forward.

Loher tightened her grip on her sword and began to draw.

I could hear Balt begin to growl from the corner of my eye and I swear I saw him slowly begin to move in for attack.

Unbeknownst to anyone, the wounds on my neck slowly began to close up and I regained some strength.

"Ladies, **ladies please**," I interrupted, gaining all attention to me, "I am **not** a vampire. It **failed**," I paused and looked directly at the huntress, "and **you** failed. Now take your precious ashes and leave."

The huntress just stood there and stared at me.

"How do you feel, McLaaud?" The knight asked as he put his hand on my shoulder.

Without taking my eyes from the huntress, I placed my hand over his, "I think I'm okay, my friend," I whispered, not believing it myself, "a little weak and dizzy, but I think I'm okay."

"You've lost a lot of blood." Brother Fost assured as he motioned for Kuchoff to pull out a non-burned chair for me.

I looked down at the puddle of my own blood that I was sitting in and became very uncomfortable; I accepted the chair Kuchoff had offered me.

I took the chair and faced it so I could sit and watch every move the vampire hunter made.

The huntress stood and stared at me for a while as I sat and stared back at her.

"Are you going to leave?" I calmly asked.

She had a mixture of concern, hate and fear in her eyes, but no answer.

I continued, "You'll have quite the fight on your hands, little Miss, if you **do** try to destroy me," I calmly stated, "Not only will I fight you, but so will my friends." I said, gesturing toward my companions. "Here's a question for a mighty vampire hunter such as yourself," I said after a moment of thought, "have you ever heard of a creature race called the olyame?"

Angelique sheepishly shook her head, frowned and then finally spoke, "I have not, should I have?"

"Come back and see me after you do," I stated, "Now go home, I think I hear your mother calling you."

"Meeka, please 'blink' him out of here and away from her." Brother Fost requested, gesturing toward the huntress.

"I'm going with you," Loher announced, "before I end up killing this little..." She let her voice trail off into a murmur.

"Anyone else?" Meeka asked as the familiar pink smoke began to swirl and surround us.

"Not I, Lassie," Balt smiled, "ta knight an' meself might 'ave a trollope te trounce, but methinks ye should take ta boy wit ye too."

"I **will** hunt you down!" I heard Angelique warn as the loud pink 'pop' took us from the 'Broken Blade' to...

⸺⸺◆⸺⸺

"Quick, Kuchoff draw those curtains closed before the vampire hunter leaves the tavern!" Meeka whispered as the pink fog quickly wafted away.

The Psionisist scrambled to the window and swiftly pulled the curtains tightly closed.

We were in my room at the inn.

I lay down on the bed and tried to rest, oddly, feeling no pain at all anywhere on or in my body.

"We'll hole up here until we know that she's gone." Loher announced in a whisper.

"How will we know when that is, Loher?" Kuchoff asked.

"I'm not quite sure yet, but I **am** sure that Balt or Quinn will look here after a while," Loher answered.

"How are you feeling, Thunor?" Brother Fost asked, wiping the sweat and some drying blood from my brow.

"I'm still weak and dizzy, but otherwise, fine." I answered with a feeble smile.

"How easily I'm forgotten," Brendt laughed as he appeared on the table next to the bed, "I'll 'blink' back to the 'Blade' and see how our favorite heroes are faring." He said.

"Tell them where we are, Brendt," Loher said. "But only after that charlatan whore is gone and far away," she paused, "or dead, whichever."

With that, the sprite winked and was away.

***

(Meanwhile, back at the 'Broken Blade'...)

"Look, I'm sure you're a nice girl when you're not hunting vampires," Sir Quinn began, "But I suggest you pack up your gear and get as far away from us as you possibly can... **Now.**"

The knight took a single step toward her with his hand resting on the hasp of his sword, "Leave the tavern owner where he is and we will make sure that he gets a proper burial."

"Aye," Balt agreed, "t'would be a shame te have ta trounce such a pretty wee Lass such as yerself, so heed ta knight's advice an' scram, b'fore anytin' else troublesome 'appens 'round 'ere."

"Your friend is now a vampire," Angelique warned, "you're going to need me. Soon."

Balt laughed, "Our priest kilt te vampire ye was chasin', lil girl, an' he healed our friend wot got bitten too. 'E's na gonna change te no blood sucker."

"And if he does," Sir Quinn added, pointing at the pile of ash left over on the floor, "Our priest is more than capable of destroying vampires, now **go!**"

The vampire hunter slowly began to pack up her gear, looking back at the corpse of the tavern owner, "You'll be sorry," she coughed, "don't say I didn't warn you." She closed the wooden case and stood to leave.

"Your warning has been noted." Sir Quinn assured as he grasped Angelique by the elbow and escorted her through the tavern door, pointed her toward the gates of town and gave a coaxing kick to her rump.

Balt and Sir Quinn stood and watched as Angelique walked through the town gates, never looking back.

"I b'lieve ta wee Lass be cryin' on ta way out ta gates." Balt laughed as he locked the tavern door.

Sir Quinn half smiled and nodded, "I don't trust her, Balt, and I don't think we've seen the last of her."

"Persistent little minx, isn't she?" Brendt offered as he appeared, perched upon Balt's helmed head.

"I donna like it, sprite," Balt admitted, "Tat wee Lass a gonna be troubles."

"I'll keep an eye on her, if you'd like." Brendt offered.

"That would be helpful, my winged friend," Sir Quinn agreed, "how goes the rest of the team?"

"Hiding safely in McLaaud's room at the inn," Brendt whispered, "they're expecting you, but be careful not to be seen going in there."

"Can you magically 'blink' us there?" The knight asked.

"One at a time, I think," The sprite answered, "I would need at least three more of me to help in order to move that ugly oaf." He laughed, pointing down, over the edge of the dwarf's helmet.

"Keep it up, Sprite," Balt growled, "err ye be me lunch!"

"Temper, temper, Balt," Sir Quinn playfully cooed, "I'm sure he was only joking."

"No." The sprite quipped as the knight and the sprite suddenly disappeared.

"Baahh," Balt growled as he removed his helmet and inspected it as if to make sure the sprite was indeed gone.

Satisfied, he returned the helmet to his head and then found himself standing with the rest of us in my room.

A few moments after that, several dozen fairies began to appear, one-by-one.

<hr>

"Brendt sent us." The fairies all sang in unison.

"What are you doing here?" Kuchoff asked with a smile as he playfully tried to capture a low flying fairie.

The fairie looped high above and flew back in for another round; she flicked the boy's ear as she passed.

"We have no choice but to report back to The Circle of Flowers that McLaaud has been bitten," The lead fairie announced, "But rest assured, they have ways of helping out unfortunate victims of vampire attacks."

"I seem to remember that from…" Loher started, slightly confused, rapidly blinking her eyes and shaking unseen cobwebs from her memory, but then, she let her voice trail off in thought.

"It was no dream, Dearie." Another fairie giggled.

"Do you mean that we were all actually **there**?" Brother Fost asked in surprise.

"Indeed, we do." A trio of fairies sang from across the room.

"Actually, to be more precise, the proper term would be *then*, not *there*." The lead fairie corrected.

"I don't understand." Brother Fost admitted.

"**There** is **here**," a fairie attempted to explain, "well, actually on the southern side of Loch Wepan, but many, many centuries from now."

"I still don't understand," Brother Fost sighed, a bit frustrated.

"Time travel, Fost," I weakly muttered, "Same place, different time. My father spoke of it often. The fairies transported us to a different time in the future, but kept us in the same place by using Natural magic, much like Meeka's unnatural 'blink' spell."

"Only better, because it's natural!" A very young fairie giggled.

"And stronger!" Another young one chimed.

"Precisely!" The lead fairie exclaimed, ignoring the youthful quips.

"Well," Balt smiled with a slap to his knee, "**Tat** explains all ta weird stuff we was seein' on ta way inta t' house!"

"Inside the house as well!" Meeka added, "I thought I knew all things magical, but those orbs and staves had me befuddled."

"Orbs and staves?" A fairie inquired.

"On the altar," the wizard answered, "the long green table."

"They call those 'billiard balls and cue sticks'," another fairie explained,

"They're part of a game."

"This is all so strange." Sir Quinn muttered in disbelief and crossed his arms.

Unexpectedly, Brendt appeared in the room with wide eyes, speaking quickly, "That vampire hunter is back in town and she looks like she means business!"

"How so?" The lead fairie inquired.

"She's asking around," the sprite continued, "asking everyone if they have seen or knows where you all are!"

"Has she gotten any leads?" Meeka asked, suddenly worried.

"None that I am aware of," Brendt answered, "But I'm sure that if she goes to the stables, the old man, Festus will know."

"She must've doubled back after ye blinked me 'ere." Balt stammered, slamming a fist into the palm of his other hand.

"Festus wouldn't give us away, would he?" Loher rhetorically asked, angry with the news.

"I'm sure he wouldn't." I reassured the elven maiden with some newfound strength, probably a dose of adrenaline due to the startling news.

"I think you should go keep a close eye on her, Brendt," Loher suggested, "Report back to us if she starts getting close, okay?"

"Right-o!" Brendt agreed with a flash and was gone.

"How soon can you get word to the witches?" I asked the lead fairie.

"We need to know if you have been turned undead first," she said, "If they put you into that chamber while you're **alive**, you won't be that way for long."

"So, we just wait 'ere until 'e d'cides te try an' **bite** one o' us?" Balt asked and then turned to me, "Sorry, ye be me Mate an' all, but I'd be forced te have te kill ye."

"Of that, my friend," I began, "I am absolutely sure. Just look what you did to poor Monty."

Balt uncontrollably began to laugh, but then cut himself short when he noticed no one else was laughing with him.

Everyone sat or stood in silence for a moment and looked from one face to another, pondering the situation and what might have to happen if, in fact, I **did** actually turn into a vampire.

"So when or how do we find out for sure if he **is** a vampire?" Brother Fost finally asked, breaking the silence.

"There **are** a few ways to find out," the lead fairie answered, "one of which is unpleasant. We have already discussed it." She nodded to the dwarf.

"What is another?" Loher inquired, dismissing any plan Balt was a part of brainstorming.

"South of here, near the town of Dournan, there is a tall tower in the Charon Swamp," the lead fairie began, "Monere Tower. Within that tower, there is an old man called Kennis. He is known to have many answers to many questions."

"I always thought that Kennis was a myth." Sir Quinn spoke up.

"Perhaps he **is**, perhaps he's not." The lead fairie said with a smile, "But know this," she said as the smile faded away and she became serious, "Monere Tower is a dangerous place. You can't just walk in there and get the answers you seek. There are perils within those walls that even Kennis himself cannot survive if he were to attempt escape."

"Escape?" Kuchoff asked.

"As I stated," the lead fairie uttered, "many perils."

"If he's even real." Another fairie added.

"They can't be any worse than the olyame." Meeka stated.

"It all depends on your own personal point of view." A fairie countered.

Unexpectedly, there was a knock on the door and everyone froze.

The fairies suddenly disappeared.

Sir Quinn and Balt readied their weapons and I tried to conceal myself as best as I could as Kuchoff went to answer the door.

"Who is it?" Kuchoff sang.

"Festus, from the stables," the voice beyond the door answered, "I need to talk to you."

Kuchoff looked back at us with a questioning look on his face.

I nodded approval, "Let him in." I said.

Kuchoff opened the door and let the old man in and then looked to see if anyone else had followed.

"I am alone and I was not followed," Festus reassured, "I had a visit from a young woman today, and she seemed very strange." He said as he stepped into the room and closed the door behind him.

We all looked at him, anxious about what might have been said.

"What did she say?" Loher asked, as if reading my mind.

Festus took a seat in one of the chairs, produced a pipe, packed it with tobacco and then lit it, puffing sweet smelling smoke about the room, "She was asking about you, McLaaud," he informed, "I told her that you have indeed boarded a horse in my stable and when she had asked which one it was, I told her it was my white mare. She would never know otherwise." He puffed some more on his pipe, "I would have told her the truth if it were not for a devious look in her eyes when she asked, so I assumed that you may be in some sort of trouble and came to investigate for myself."

"And you're sure you weren't followed." Loher nudged.

"Quite sure, my Lady," Festus began, "I've grown up and grown old within these walls. I know my way around these grounds better than the young King himself."

"I'm no Lady." Loher spat.

"Sure you are," Festus laughed, "you're all Lords and Ladies as long as you're wearing those golden pins the King gave you."

I smiled at the old man, "You have done me a great justice, Festus, and I am forever in your debt." I breathed.

"You can start to repay that debt by telling me what this is all about, my Lord." Festus said, sinking down into the chair and hanging his left ankle over his right knee; his puffing continued.

"In order for you to completely understand, we will have to start at the beginning." I said.

"That's as good of a place as any." Festus laughed.

"As you may already know, we were sent to investigate a new cave in the Haze Cove." I began.

"I was unaware of that, but I'm assuming that is the reason for your royal pins, please continue." The old man smiled.

"Perhaps we should tell just the important parts about the vampire," Brother Fost added, "and about being bitten."

"Vampire?" Festus asked with wide eyes, "Bitten?"

"Yes," I admitted, "the girl that came to you asking questions about me is a vampire hunter named Angelique DeStruere."

"So, you're a vampire?" Festus asked as he sat up straight in his chair.

I raised a calming hand and tried to smile, "We don't know yet. I was just bitten about two hours ago, but Brother Fost healed me right away and the vampire that bit me has been destroyed."

"Which reminds me," Sir Quinn said as a thought, "Lance is still lying dead on the bar. We should go give him a proper burial."

"The vampire killed Lance?" Festus asked with a waver in his voice.

"Unfortunately." Loher spat coldly.

Festus sat bolt upright in his chair once again, wide eyed and concerned, "Is there a chance that **he** could become a vampire?"

"Nah," Balt answered, unsure, "'E was a goner as soon as 'is throat was torn out."

Festus grimaced at that thought. "Why did the vampire attack Lance?"

"Lance attacked first, shot at it with the crossbow he keeps behind the bar," Meeka informed, "but the vampire wore a chest plate under its clothes to protect its heart and the bolt bounced off."

"Why was the vampire after you, McLaaud?" Festus asked.

"McLaaud spoiled ta bloodsucker's dinner plans." Balt chuckled.

No one else found his joke funny.

Meeka shot him a look of distaste.

Balt frowned and slightly hung his head in mock shame.

"We need to get out of town without being noticed by Angelique," I began, "she's after **me** now because she thinks **I'm** infected."

Festus sat there for a moment, puffing on his pipe thoughtfully, "I think I have a plan," he said, eyeing Sir Quinn and I, "but, in order for this to work, you and the knight have to exchange armor."

"Why?" Sir Quinn asked.

"Just trust me on this. I'll be back in an hour." Festus said as he got up and exited the room.

CHAPTER TWO
CAT & MOUSE

An hour later, Festus showed up back at the inn, whistling a jaunty tune.

Sir Quinn and I had exchanged our armor; mine was a bit tight on him and I was having trouble keeping his on straight.

"The vampire hunter broke into 'The Blade' and took Lance," Festus announced quietly, "I saw her carrying the body as I passed on my way back to the stables."

"Na more mister nice guy," Balt growled, "Next time I sees 'er, I'm gonna..."

Meeka placed her hand on Balt's shoulder to calm him down; the warrior stopped.

"So," I said, drawing attention to myself, "What exactly **is** the plan, Festus?"

"I have strategically parked two covered wagons set with your mounts on each," Festus explained, "Sir Quinn and I are going to take a walk to the stables, making sure the vampire hunter sees us on the way. She will believe that Sir Quinn is you, McLaaud, that way she follows him, keeping the rest of you clear as you get to the covered wagons and get safely out of town. Sir Quinn will then take my white mare and ride out of town in the opposite direction, and get onto the other ferry."

"I understand the plan now!" Sir Quinn exclaimed, "We will then meet up in a few days after she finds out that she has been tricked and I lose her in the forest."

"Precisely, good Sir Knight!" Festus laughed.

Meeka got a worried look on her face, "What happens if she tries to kill you, Quinn?" She asked.

"I'll take care of that!" Kuchoff stammered excitedly, "I have a spell all ready for this very occasion that I have been waiting to try out!"

"Do you mean that it has never been tested?" Sir Quinn asked nervously.

"On a watermelon." The boy answered.

"What 'appened wit ta melon?" Balt inquired.

"I ate it." Kuchoff said, licking his lips and smiling.

"I'm sure you'll be fine, Sir Knight." Brother Fost laughed.

Sir Quinn grumbled a bit and then finally agreed.

"It's almost nightfall," Loher announced.

"Is everybody ready?" Festus asked.

"As ready as we'll ever be." The knight sighed and began to gather his gear.

"Alright, Sir Quinn," Festus said, "let's get moving, the rest of you stay put until you see Sir Quinn ride out followed by the vampire hunter. One of the covered wagons is behind the inn and to the south; the other is west of here beyond the churchyard."

Kuchoff grabbed Sir Quinn's hand, "Kneel down for a moment, I need to cast the spell," he urged.

Sir Quinn reluctantly complied with the child's request.

"Cor scutum." Kuchoff incanted as he placed his small hand on Sir Quinn's broad chest.

Sir Quinn was almost knocked back from the force of the spell but he caught his balance and quickly stood up with a shocked look on his face that slowly turned into a smile, "Thank you, my mysterious little friend," Sir Quinn smiled, "I have no doubt that this spell is going to work!"

Kuchoff smiled back, "Good luck." He giggled.

"I'll see you all in Dournan in a few days." The knight said as he left.

"I guess it's 'Hurry up and wait' time." Kuchoff said as he scampered across the room and cautiously peered out of the window to watch the stableman and the knight dressed in ranger's clothing disappear around a corner.

Soon after, the vampire hunter slipped around the same corner as planned.

"Wot now?" Balt rhetorically asked as he gathered up his own gear and placed it all near the door.

It was beginning to grow darker outside as the sun slowly dipped down behind the castle.

"I hope Sir Quinn will be safe." Meeka sighed as she slumped onto the bed next to Loher, who was also slumped on the bed next to me.

"He said it himself," Kuchoff chirped, "my spell is gonna work."

"I'm wonderin' meself if 'e's gonna be able te lose ta lil vamp hunter as easily as Festus tinks 'e is." Balt added, inspecting the blade on his Great Axe.

Moments later, Sir Quinn, disguised as me, trotted past our window on Festus' white mare; the knight made the horse nicker as he strode by.

Less than a minute later, after the knight passed through the town gates, Angelique the vampire hunter stealthily rode past the window as well, quickening her pace.

"There she goes," Kuchoff reported, "right on time and just as the old man expected."

"Perhaps she is not as smart as we had feared." Brother Fost stated as he rose from his chair and grabbed his gear.

"Don't underestimate her, Fost," Loher warned as she paced the floor, "she may be letting us think that she's following the plans, while in fact she is setting a trap for McLaaud to fall into."

"Well then," Meeka giggled, "it's a good thing that you're so good at disarming traps, isn't it?"

"Besides," I added, "She'll have no idea which wagon I get into, if she even knows about one or both of the wagons."

"Unless she was watching Festus park the wagons and kept an eye on him as he came to our room." Loher warned again.

"I'm sure he was careful not to be followed," I stated, "He wouldn't jeopardize his own plan."

"Let's just take the escape tat ta old man gived us and get out o' 'ere while we 'ave ta chance." Balt stated as he walked to the door and grabbed up his gear.

The rest of us followed the dwarf as we left the inn.

We split up once we made it to the street, Brother Fost, Loher and I went one way, while Meeka, Kuchoff and Balt went the other.

"We'll be seein' ye." Balt shot over his shoulder as he and his team swiftly walked away toward the churchyard.

My team and I walked around the corner and found our covered wagon sitting there with my black roan stallion, 'Stahvee', Loher's appaloosa mare, 'Amarylis' and Sir Quinn's appaloosa gelding, 'Sicuro' hitched to the wagon as a team.

Tied up to the rear of the wagon was an unfamiliar grey pleven and Kuchoff's spotted pony, 'Mannulus.'

"Ahh," a female voice from the driver's seat sighed, "I see that you have finally arrived as Festus said that you would."

"Show yourself!" I hissed as I drew my sword; Loher quickly drew her own.

The shadow in the driver's seat slowly pulled her hood back, revealing the face of the female half of the elven lovers from the 'Ale House' in the dwarven town of Dewarg and the 'Broken Blade' here in the Royal City, Salvus Hus.

"My husband and I are stable hands for Festus," she explained, "We are to drive your two teams safely out of the city to wherever you decide to go. I'm assuming by your reaction to me being here that you are probably in some sort of trouble and we probably don't have much time, so get in, you can explain on the way if you choose to do so. The only thing I really need to know is where we are going; the rest is up to you."

"We need you to follow that girl at a very safe distance," Loher explained as we climbed into the wagon, "Don't let her know we are following her."

"Will do." The driver said with a smile as she turned around and coaxed the horses into motion.

***

Balt, Meeka and Kuchoff made their way among the headstones of the churchyard, pausing briefly for Kuchoff to catch up, as he had become distracted by a name on one of the headstones.

"Did you know who that was?" Meeka asked as the boy caught up.

"The name looked familiar, but it wasn't who I thought it was," he answered.

"Who'd ye tink it was, Boy-o?" Balt inquired.

"My mother," Kuchoff answered with a slight crack in his voice, "But the dates were too old to be her."

"Perhaps t'was your grammutter?" Balt replied.

"Your mother might not be dead, Sweetheart," Meeka sighed as she placed her hand lovingly upon the boy's shoulder and drew him closer to her side.

"Ta wagon be sittin' right where Festus said it'd be." Balt announced pointing his finger across the yard.

The trio quickened their pace and arrived at the wagon moments later.

"You must be the folks I'm waiting for," a male elf announced as he stroked the mane of one of the horses hitched to the front of the covered wagon, "I work for Festus, and he told me to escort you out of town and take you to wherever the other wagon is going to meet up with you."

"Juss 'ead outta town an' go south." Balt relayed as he helped Meeka and Kuchoff into the wagon and then climbed in after them.

"South Port Royale it is then," the elven driver said as he coaxed the team of horses into motion with a slight whip crack over their heads.

"Driver," Meeka called, tapping him on his arm, "We are heading to Dournan, but don't go directly there, we are trying to lose someone."

"Understood," the driver acknowledged, "I'm assuming it would be that little human girl with the big wooden box."

"That would be her!" Kuchoff confirmed.

"You don't have to worry about her," the driver relayed, "She followed a guy on a white horse out of town a few moments ago. I believe my wife and your friends followed her shortly after."

"Donna take no chances, Mate," Balt delivered, "We trust 'er 'bout as far as ta boy 'ere kin toss 'er in ta air."

"Understood." The driver repeated and then turned back to the horses.

Kuchoff giggled and pulled Balt closer, "With my Psi-skills, I probably **could** toss her into the air," he whispered.

"I be fargett'n 'bout them skills 'o' yers, Boy." The dwarf admitted.

The wagons exited the town of Salvus Hus from opposite exits and each headed for opposite ports.

Night was closing in fast, which meant that there was more cover for us to hide from the vampire hunter.

Both parties began to relax a bit as we slowly headed out of town.

I'm quite sure that all of our thoughts were on the knight, Sir Quinn.

———— ◆ ————

"Excellent," Sir Quinn thought, as he glanced over his own shoulder and saw the vampire hunter following him at a distance as he rode out of the Royal town of Salvus Hus.

Festus' white mare was healthy and strong and kept up the pace longer than the knight had expected her to.

North Port Royale was just within sight as the sun completely dipped down below the peaks of the Ferrum Mons.

The ferryman was just about to remove the drawbridge that connected the dock to the ferry when he saw Sir Quinn riding hard to make it on time, "Come on, Boy, I'll wait for you! You almost missed the last one out!"

"I appreciate your waiting for me," Sir Quinn said as he led his horse onto the ferry, "The next rider is chasing me for nefarious reasons, but I would appreciate it if we could wait for her as well." Sir Quinn stated as he handed the ferryman a handful of coins.

The ferryman's eyes went wide at the weight of gold, "Absolutely, me Lord!" He cried in delight and then, he realized what Sir Quinn had told him, so his face twisted in confusion.

"The less you ask, the less trouble you bring on yourself." Sir Quinn said to the ferryman before he could ask a single word.

The ferryman just smiled and nodded, patting his gold-filled purse.

A few moments later, the vampire hunter arrived on the dock with an evil smile upon her beautiful face and boarded the ferry with no word.

She casually dropped a gold coin onto the deck to pay the ferryman.

The ferryman pulled back the drawbridge and set the vessel on its way.

The knight intently watched the vampire hunter board the ferry and the drawbridge raised before he mixed himself into the crowd.

He hoped it would take a while, but not too long for her to find him... and the mistake she had made.

⚬

"There goes the last ferry of the night," The female elven driver announced as we approached North Port Royale.

"Can you see our friend and the huntress aboard?" Brother Fost asked.

The driver leaned forward and squinted her eyes, "I can see the girl, but... Yes, I see your friend with the white horse. They are both aboard." She announced.

"I sure hope he's going to be okay." Brother Fost worried out loud.

I have to admit that I was quite worried for his safety as well, even with Kuchoff's protection spell cast upon his heart.

Human hearts are far different than watermelons, but the boy has proven time and time again that he knew what he was doing with those Psi-skills, so I had no choice, but to trust him with Sir Quinn's life... as well as my own.

Loher just sat there, holding my hand looking quite worried as well, but I'm sure it was not just for the knight's safety.

"I'm willing to believe she won't try anything on such a crowded ferry." I commented, trying to make the priest feel a bit more at ease.

As soon as the ferry was all but a lantern's flame on the horizon, the driver announced, "I suggest we set up camp here by the dock, that way we can get on the first ferry to the mainland, tomorrow and get you to where you all need to go."

"Agreed." Loher said as she began to gather our gear and get out of the wagon.

"You stay here on the wagon, Thunor." Brother Fost said as he climbed over the side of the wagon, "I'll bring you some food, are you hungry?"

"Starving!" I answered, "I can't remember the last time I have ever been so hungry!"

"You lost a lot of blood and your body is just trying to compensate for the loss, that's all it is." The priest assured.

I was wide-awake now, full of energy and not wanting to stay hidden in the wagon, "Brother Fost," I called, "I feel fine. Better than fine, I feel great!" I said excitedly.

"Are you sure?" Loher asked.

"The threat is with Sir Quinn on that ferry," I said, pointing toward the dock, "I'm coming out of here to help with camp."

Brother Fost smiled and agreed, "I guess you're right, my friend, but if you start to feel..."

"I'll be alright." I said, cutting him off.

I climbed out of the wagon and stood there, looking around for a moment.

The nighttime world looked somewhat brighter than I was used to, even with my infrared elven sight.

My stomach was growling and I could not keep my mind off of the hunger I felt.

I helped Brother Fost gather firewood while Loher and the wagon driver went out to hunt for food.

Moments later, the two women came back to camp with a line full of fish with arrows protruding from their bodies and a small, but fat wild turkey.

Brother Fost was impressed and excited at the sight of all of those fish, while I was eyeing up the turkey.

By the time the fire was down to cooking embers, we had the turkey plucked and dressed with local herbs, and the fish were cleaned and gutted.

Less than an hour later we were devouring the fish while the turkey continued to cook; it was giving off the most wonderful fragrance and was making my stomach sing even after the fact that I had eaten more fish than ever before.

We sat and exchanged stories with the wagon driver whose name turned out to be Zeepha H'Oadd.

We introduced ourselves as well, mentioning the others on her husband's wagon.

She told us that her husband's name is Quendonipa H'Oadd and that they had been married only a very short time, but had known each other almost their whole entire lives.

They had met early on in life at school and then, later, due to a war between the elves and the hobgoblins, they had lost track of each other.

Decades had gone past and she had gone on with her life with little-to-no thought about him during that time; in fact, she had gone ahead and taken a husband, but he had ignored her and refused to give her a child.

Though he did not necessarily treat her badly, she was quite unhappy with him and eventually they split up with the blessings of the elven elders.

Quendonipa, on the other hand, had always kept Zeepha within his thoughts throughout the years, but with no reason to believe that they would ever be reunited. He too had taken a wife and fathered a child, a daughter that had been taken away in the night by her mother as she had found a new love and decided to leave.

The elven elders granted Quendonipa annulment of his vows and promised that when the time came and the child was found, she would go to her father; the waiting continues.

Zeepha told us that a little over a year ago, Quendonipa had returned to their village in the Seolfer Wudu, and that they had met up in the market, at the hand of a mutual friend; they rekindled their relationship with each other and it has only grown stronger as time has gone by.

They have happily been together ever since and had actually gotten lawfully married with the elven elders blessings only a few weeks ago.

"Such a lovely story," Brother Fost stated as he checked the progress of the cooking turkey, "The turkey is almost ready."

"I'm ready to eat!" I said excitedly and rose to my feet.

"Ladies first, my eager friend!" Brother Fost chuckled and poked at me with a stick.

I laughed it off and waited my turn for the luscious, succulent meat that tormented my senses for more than three hours.

The turkey was finally served and it tasted so good.

The meat went down my throat as if it was greased; I hardly had to chew.

I looked up at the others as we ate and I noticed that Loher was staring at me with an odd, almost fearful look on her face, but before I could ask what was wrong, she shrugged it off and continued eating.

That hunger!

Could **nothing** satisfy it?

The turkey was suddenly gone, yet I was still craving...

...Craving, something **more!**

After we ate, a jug of wine was passed from friend to friend.

It tasted awful, like vinegar to me, yet no one else seemed to mind.

I found this strange, so I got up to go for a walk.

"Are you okay?" Brother Fost asked with a twinge of worry in his voice.

"Yes, quite fine," I lied, "I just thought I would stretch out my legs for a bit. That wagon was most uncomfortable."

"Would you like me to go with you?" Loher asked.

"No, Dear, I'll be alright by myself, you stay here and relax." I told her.

———— ◆ ————

South Port Royale was bustling with excitement as Balt, Meeka and Kuchoff's covered wagon pulled onto the dock.

It seems that there were already vampire stories floating to the mainland and a large group of vampire hunters were arriving by the boatful.

"Tiss cuid mean a bit o' trouble." Balt stated under his breath.

"Perhaps we should do something." Meeka suggested.

"Like wot, Lass?" Balt asked a bit annoyed.

"I don't know," she stammered, "tell them that the vampire has already been destroyed?"

The dwarf and the wizard just stood there, staring at each other for what must have seemed like an eternity.

"I have an idea." Kuchoff finally announced.

Balt and Meeka turned to look at the boy.

Kuchoff suddenly jumped out of the wagon and bounded to a pile of loose dirt.

He scooped up a large portion of the material and poured it into a sack from somewhere within his robes.

After this feat was completed, he ran back to the wagon with the sack of dry dirt.

"What are you going to do with that?" Meeka asked.

He handed the sack to Balt and said, "Get everyone's attention and then slowly pour this out into the water, Meeka, you tell them that the vampire has already been destroyed, wave your hands around like you destroyed it with a spell or something and I'll do the rest!"

Kuchoff had already used his Psi-skills a few times in the past and proved that he could make people and intelligent creatures such as dragons believe things that just simply were not real.

For example, (recap) he had once tricked a young dragon named Kusagi, into believing that it was really seeing and speaking to the king of all dragons, Lord Avilyn, while it was actually Kuchoff altering reality by using that skill.

Balt and Meeka climbed out of the wagon and proceeded to the middle of the commotion while Kuchoff stayed on the sidelines and prepared his own part of the plan.

Meeka suddenly got the idea to conjure up a small cloud of the familiar pink smoke that she had used a few times before as well, in order to gather everyone's attention.

As the cloud of pink smoke dissipated, she began to speak, "The vampire has already been destroyed!" She called, waving her hands in the air while puffing out more tiny clouds of pink smoke from thin air.

"Prove it!" Members of the crowd began to shout.

Meeka nodded at Balt, who in turn began to pour the dirt from the sack into the water.

In the quickly dissipating light, the material that flowed from the sack was a chalky grey color instead of the normal brownish tan color of dirt, and the dust that separated from the material wafted upon the wind like that of burned ash.

The spectacle was actually quite convincing as the vampire hunters gathered around and let the 'ash' flow through their fingers and drop down into the water.

Once the sack was empty, most of the vampire hunters turned away, satisfied and boarded their boats and returned back to the mainland or wherever else they had come from; the dock was slowly being vacated.

By the time the sun had completely dipped down below the distant peaks of the Ferrum Mons, the last ferry of the day's final call to the mainland was announced and the team was ushered aboard.

The voyage to South Ferian Harbor was interesting yet uneventful to say the least.

It was much too dark to enjoy the view so attention was given to the travelers on board.

Many of them were vampire hunters and their assistants, while others were townsfolk that either worked on the island or came to see the castle.

Talk of vampires dominated the conversations and the team had heard quite a few different ways to dispose of the nefarious creatures, some of which were probably untrue.

Moments later, as the ferry arrived, South Ferian Harbor was also a bustle of energy that was slowly growing weaker as word that the vampire had finally been destroyed was passed around.

Small clusters of cheers rose up from the crowd here and there, as the crowd began to thin out and return from whence they came.

Occasionally, small groups of people would congratulate Meeka and the rest as they all believed that she was the one that destroyed the vampire herself.

Besides the unwanted attention, the team was careful to keep to themselves as they snaked their way through the crowd and exited the harbor area.

Once out on the path, they began to relax a bit more as they purposely passed the path that went west to Dournan and continued to go south and then east to the bridge that led to Swapton, the large trading town.

⸺⸺◆⸺⸺

The vampire hunter slowly walked up behind Sir Quinn as he casually looked out at the darkness over the side of the ferry as it made its way to North Ferian Harbor, "It looks to me that your friends decided to push you out of their little team now that you're changing," Angelique laughed, believing that she was speaking to me and not Sir Quinn, "How does it feel? Painful?"

Sir Quinn quickly whipped around and gently placed the edge of a dagger's blade across the young girl's throat, a lock of golden blond hair fell from her shoulder to the deck, "Not as painful as this blade is going to feel if you don't leave my friends and myself alone," the knight smiled, showing his teeth, "You got the wrong guy, vampire hunter. You sure are bad at your job, little girl and furthermore, if you're going to sneak up on someone to kill them, you should keep your damn mouth shut and just kill them. Words are cheap and useless to the dead."

Angelique's eyes went wide and filled with sudden fear as she realized her potentially fatal mistake.

After a long moment of staring her down, Sir Quinn relaxed his grip on the blade and let the girl go with a forceful backward shove.

The girl went down hard to the deck and even landed with a slight bounce, quite like a sack of old, rotting potatoes.

"I **will** find your friend," Angelique said as she regained her composure and checked her throat for blood, "I'll call in a team of hunters if I have to. You can't stop all of us!"

"Or I could just kill you now. You just never give up, do you?" Sir Quinn chuckled, "Normally, I would find that to be an honorable trait, especially in a girl of your age, but this time, not so much." The knight sheathed his dagger and bit down on a piece of dried meat he had found in a pocket. "You should know that you've already lost him." he proudly stated as he turned back to the railing and gazed again into the darkness.

"But I haven't lost you." She smugly countered.

The knight slowly turned around again with his hand on the hasp of his sword, "Did my warning to leave us alone mean **nothing** to you?"

"I don't respond well to threats," she answered.

"That was no threat, little girl, that was a promise." He said, unblinking.

The night sky was a brilliant sea of stars that looked twice as large as it was reflected off of the now still, glasslike surface of Loch Regalis.

The air was alive with the sounds of nocturnal creatures as they chirped, hummed and croaked in natural harmony.

Small bats swooped silently about to collect tiny flying insects for their dinner while off in the distance, a small pack of wolves cried out to the moon.

Everything seemed so peaceful, except for the undying hunger I was feeling.

I had eaten more in my last meal than I could ever remember eating at any time before and yet the hunger still plagued my body like a disease.

I had to feed... on blood, and I was beginning to not care whose blood it was.

Instinctually, I snatched a bat from the air and sank my teeth into the warm, furry flesh.

It wasn't enough.

One more bat became two, then three.

By the time I was satisfied, the corpses of over a dozen bats and a few rats lay dead at my feet.

I stood there for what seemed like an hour trying to collect my thoughts and then slowly walked back to the camp.

Brother Fost was in the wagon, fast asleep while Loher and Zeepha were softly chatting next to the fire.

"I was beginning to worry about you," Loher said as I walked into the camp and sat on the other side of the fire, "We were just contemplating going to look for you."

"I'm fine," I lied again and half smiled.

"Aren't you tired yet?" Zeepha asked.

"No," I answered, "Not yet."

Loher shot me another worried look, held it there for a moment and then turned to continue her conversation with Zeepha.

They chatted together into the night while I sat and watched shooting stars caress the heavens.

I could hear night creatures playing and hunting in the forest behind me and secretly wished I was out there too.

It wouldn't be long until I had to feel that dreadful hunger once again.

The sun finally began to peek out from below the horizon and the morning birds began to sing in tune as the night sounds slowly died away.

Brother Fost stirred me from my thoughts, "How are you doing, Thunor?" The priest asked.

"Hungry." I said without thinking.

"Strange," the priest thought out loud, "You ate so much last night, how can this be?"

"The hunger is not going away." I reported.

"How long has this been going on?" He asked.

"Just last night and now today." I answered.

The halfling priest placed his left hand on my head and his right hand on my belly.

He then closed his eyes and began to chant in the halfling tongue.

Mere seconds later, I felt a sharp twinge within my guts and then felt nothing.

"How do you feel now?" He asked.

"Better." I smiled. "The hunger is gone. What did you do?"

"Simply healed you," he whispered, also with a smile, "I'm afraid it's only temporary though."

"Is he okay, Brother Fost?" Loher asked as she invited herself into the conversation.

"Quite fine, my Dear, quite fine." The priest conveyed.

"He has not slept a wink." She said.

"You'll be good to remember, Loher," Brother Fost began with a slight hint of sternness in his words, "He **is** half elven, so sleep is a bit of an optional past time for him, just as it is for you."

"The team of horses is all hitched up, friends," Zeepha announced, "The first ferry is well on its way." She said, pointing to the dock.

Off in the distance, we could see the ferry moving swiftly across the water toward us.

We all gathered up our gear and climbed aboard the wagon, staying hidden, just in case the vampire hunter should ask anyone if they had seen us or worse yet, if she's on that boat herself.

Moments later, we were aboard the ferry and on our way to North Ferian Harbor.

We were the only passengers aboard, so we slipped out of the wagon to stretch our legs and walk around a bit, still staying well out of the sight of the ferryman.

It was turning into a bright sunny day, a little too warm for me, but no one else complained about the new summer heat.

It had been a long cold winter before we set out to explore and chart that new cave, in fact, there was still frost on the ground as I set out from my home in the Seolfer Wudu and traveled to the castle for the very first time.

It seemed so long ago as I stood there, gazing at the wave-less water that surrounded the island upon which the castle sat.

I looked in the direction that we were traveling and began to see the tops of trees take shape, so I reluctantly climbed back into the wagon and hid myself for the last leg of the journey.

We could not afford to have me seen in case the huntress decided to wait there at the dock once she discovered that she was actually chasing Sir Quinn and not me.

Thoughts of the old man in the tower kept me focused on hopes that this would be over soon.

The only thing that plagued my mind now was where were Brendt and the fairies?

The trading town of Swapton was just waking up along with the rising sun.

A distant rooster was making its first wakeup call as the wagon carrying Balt, Meeka and Kuchoff arrived through the gates of the town.

Children of various ages were already playing in the streets and poor beggars had their hands out.

Swapton was the largest established town in the realm of Beornan Heafod. It stretched on for almost as far as the eye could see and was arguably larger than the whole of Salvus Hus, including the castle.

In fact, it was a Metropolis with several large stone buildings surrounded by hundreds of residential homes that were not made of simple wood, straw and mud, but were built to last with stone and mortar.

The thing that made Swapton so great was its location; almost directly in the center of the mainland and half way between the castle and the elven homeland, the Seolfer Wudu.

Many paths led to and from this town, so it was a hub for travelers either going to or coming from the castle, making it a prime location for purchase, trade and even crime, unfortunately.

A common saying associated with Swapton was: 'If Swapton doesn't have it, it probably doesn't exist and keep your purse close.'

The wagon pulled up to the inn and tavern in the town square.

Balt, Meeka and Kuchoff scrambled out of the wagon and dusted themselves off.

"Methinks we should keep te ourselves whilst 'ere and go te get us some eats." Balt suggested.

"I agree," Meeka said as she combed a knot out of Kuchoff's hair with her fingers.

"If I didn't know any better," Quendonipa observed, "I'd swear that you two were mother and son."

Kuchoff looked up at Meeka and smiled, Meeka smiled back, "It's almost as if we are." Meeka stated and then kissed Kuchoff on the top of the head.

Balt smiled and laughed as he turned to enter the tavern.

The tavern here in Swapton, aptly named: 'The Trading Post,' was just opening back up for the day's business.

Coffee and fresh fried eggs were on Meeka's mind as they sat at the same table they always sat at in any tavern they found themselves.

Balt ordered a large mug of honey ale and a portion of beef from the night before, while Kuchoff ordered a couple of eggs and some milk.

Quendonipa stood apart from the trio and took his meal of fresh bread back out to the wagon to watch and feed the horses and think about Zeepha; he was quite content with that and smiled the whole time.

Little by little, the town began to come alive as shops began to open and peddlers sold their wares to passersby on the streets.

The streets became crowded as merchants and patrons alike moved from shop to shop.

The trio finished their breakfast and exited the tavern just in time to catch a pickpocket attempt to swipe a coin purse from an unsuspecting victim standing in line to buy some vegetables from a stand.

"I wouldn't do that if I were you." Kuchoff said in a loud voice.

The thief looked up at him and stopped what she was doing; as did the man standing in line.

The man that was about to be robbed became very angry and balled up his fist to strike the female thief.

"I wouldn't do **that** if I were you." Kuchoff repeated; a sharp glare in his eyes.

<hr>

North Ferian Harbor was a dark and gloomy place in the wee hours of the early morning.

Not a soul but the harbor master was in sight.

The travelers from the ferry disembarked one by one and followed the path away and out of sight.

Finally Sir Quinn and the huntress led their horses off onto solid ground and just stood there staring at each other for a while.

"I'm going to Carrington now," Sir Quinn said, "You're welcome to join me."

Angelique looked around at the barren harbor area.

"That was the last ferry of the night, Angelique," Sir Quinn quietly said, "You might as well come with me, you're going to follow me anyway."

She continued to look around, not saying a word.

"Have it your way," Sir Quinn sighed as he mounted Festus' white mare and nudged it along the path a few feet and then stopped and looked over his shoulder; the vampire hunter was gone! "I should have just killed her when I had the chance, but still, I wonder where she disappeared to." He thought to himself and then strode off toward Carrington.

The night was darker than Sir Quinn had ever seen and he wondered if it was only his imagination, because he **knew** that Angelique was following him.

"Why didn't she join me? There is safety in numbers and she knows I know she's back there following me. How stupid does she think I am?" He rhetorically asked the white mare out loud, "She's more foolish than I thought."

The white horse just nickered out her untranslatable reply and they trotted on in silence, at a good steady pace, toward the sleepy little town of Carrington.

The sun was just about to rise when he arrived.

⚬

"The King makes us pay taxes for these roads, right?" Brother Fost asked, breaking the unnerving silence.

"That's what we're told," Zeepha answered, "although, the money goes for other things too; why do you ask?"

"These roads are terrible," the priest uncharacteristically complained, "with all of this bouncing, we're all going to end up with hemorrhoids, or worse."

Zeepha and Loher began to smile and outwardly laugh as the halfling finally noticed the woven straw cushions the pair of women were sat upon.

"You're being unusually quiet, Thunor," Brother Fost inquired as we were finally out of sight of the harbor.

"It's cool and comfortable here in the shade." I responded, shielding my eyes from the sun.

Zeepha and Loher gave each other quick confused glances and then looked back at me; Brother Fost quickly climbed into the back with me and told Zeepha to pay attention to the team of horses.

She complied, but Loher began to look worried.

"He **is** infected by that vampire's bite isn't he, Fost?" Loher excitedly cried.

"Calm down, Loher, I'm fine," I spat, "I'm just tired, that's all. I'm not used to not sleeping enough yet."

"I assure you my dear elven maiden," the priest calmed, "If there is something wrong, I will cure it, now please do not attract so much attention to the cover and safety of this wagon."

Loher scowled in frustration and reluctantly turned around forward to save face.

Zeepha returned Loher's attention to the woven seat cushions, which made Loher release a small grin and a slight chuckle.

Brother Fost rubbed his sore buttocks in defiance and then settled down into a soft, spare wagon cover that was folded on the floor, comfortable at last.

About an hour later, we could see some small wooden structures on the path ahead.

"The town of Carrington is just over the crest of the next hill," Zeepha announced, "Should we stop there, or continue on to Swapton, which is about another half day's journey more to the south?"

"Continue on to Swapton," I weakly replied before anyone else, "We're in a covered wagon delivering our wares to the trading town, besides, we have no business in Carrington and that is probably where our foe followed Sir Quinn anyway. At least that's where I would go to lose someone trailing me, a crowd."

"What if the guards look in the wagon and see no wares to sell?" Zeepha asked.

"We're not selling wares then," Brother Fost corrected, "we shall tell them that McLaaud here is sick and we need to see their doctor or surgeon."

"That makes perfect sense to me." Loher added.

"Okay," Zeepha agreed, "Swapton it is."

⸻ ◆ ⸻

"What do you think you're going to do about it, child?" The angry man asked in an attacking tone.

"Not he," Balt countered as he stepped out from behind the wagon with his Great Axe in hand, "It be **me,**" he said as he took a slight step toward the man, "Yer purse be saved by ta child an' yer life can now be saved by yerself. Me axe 'ere 'as na eaten yet tis foin, foin marnin' so me tinks ye shud be on yer ways, ta both of ya, b'fore me axe 'ere d'cides te take a bite'r two."

Without hesitation, the man and the thief went off quickly in two different directions as Balt and Kuchoff watched and laughed.

"Donna do tat again, Boy-o," Balt suddenly turned and said sternly, "I sez te not bring no attention te ourselves fer a reason, an' tat be it. Now we haveta move along wit not a piece o' rest fer ta harses."

"I'm sorry Balt." Kuchoff apologized with a slight frown.

"Narmally, it'd be a guid ting ya did there, so donna feel te badly 'bout it." Balt said soothingly and roughly patted the boy on the back.

Kuchoff giggled, smiled again and punched Balt in the arm, which made Balt feign pain and playfully grasped it with his other hand and say 'Ow!'

A playful battle between the two escalated in the street, causing quite the stir and gaining a lot of unwanted attention.

When a few guards began to show a bit of attention, the pair of 'warriors' decided enough was enough.

The two of them laughed as they climbed back into the wagon with Meeka and Quendonipa.

With a light snap of the reigns, the horses slowly began to head out of town.

"Where to?" Quendonipa asked casually over his shoulder.

"Dournan." Meeka carefully whispered.

Quendonipa smiled and urged the team of horses into a nice, easy trot.

As the knight continued through the gates of the town called Carrington, the sun was low in the sky, casting long shadows about the town, which vaguely reminded him of his boyhood home, the town of Herostun.

The town was small, much too small for a knight to reside in, made up of roughly built homes and barns made up of straw, grass, and mud and if you were lucky enough, wood.

The residents were all peasants and farmers, uneducated and poor.

Carrington was less than a town per/se, rather, a collective of people that long ago gathered together for safety's sake and became a lasting community.

This town was the closest that anyone cared to be to the castle and still remain free from constant rule and tyranny while the old King reigned.

There was no lordly manor or stately home.

No one governed the people that resided there and oddly enough, there was little or no crime.

Things have changed for the better, now that King Lagu Ofer'Eal has been on the throne.

Most of the people around here agree that the old King's young son is a far better and much nicer ruler.

Taxes have been lowered and the threats of orc and hobgoblin invasions have decreased significantly within the past two months, due to the roaming troops of Royal Soldiers.

Even more and more trading wagons on their way to and from Swapton, the neighboring town, stop in at almost regular intervals creating commerce and trade within the tiny commune.

Life was slowly getting better in the sleepy town of Carrington and the knight could almost feel it as he rode into town.

"You there, good man," Sir Quinn called out to a man on the road, "Could you direct me to a place where I can feed and water my horse?"

"I'll be happy to do it if you'll pay me, m'lord!" The man smiled a toothless grin.

"Will I be able to eat there as well?" The knight asked.

"We don't have much, m'lord, but you're welcome to it for gold!" The man grinned again.

"Some gold I have," Sir Quinn smiled, "Food and comfort for my horse and myself, I don't."

"I have some oats and some bread, wine and cheese, m'lord." The man whispered as the knight climbed down and handed him the horse's reigns.

"That all sounds like a feast to us" Sir Quinn said as he patted the horse's neck.

The man held out his hand for payment in advance.

"You didn't happen to see my sister come through here earlier, did you?" The knight asked as he held up three gold coins.

"That blond beauty ain't yer sister, m'lord, but she's over in that there barn watching for someone. Must be you." The man said with a casual nod of his head to show the general direction of the vampire hunter's whereabouts.

Sir Quinn simply smiled and thanked him, dropping the coins in the man's hand.

"Trouble, she is, m'lord," the man shivered, "Death follows her wherever she goes."

"How do you know all of this?" Sir Quinn asked, quite astonished.

"I could see it in her eyes, m'lord," he said as he led the knight into his barn, "Up to no good, that girl is, if I was you, and I'm glad I ain't, I'd be a might bit careful 'round the likes o' her."

"Thanks for the warning," Sir Quinn smiled, "I'll try to remember that."

—⊰◦⊱—

The ride to Swapton was quite uneventful, but when we arrived in Swapton, a group of guards stopped us at the gate.

As expected.

They told us that they were looking for a dwarf with an axe and a young human boy who had caused a disturbance here earlier, and that the wagon they had left in resembled the one we were in.

We told them that I was sick and we needed to see a doctor immediately.

The guards accepted our story and pointed us in the correct direction to find a doctor.

When we were far enough away from the guards, Brother Fost began to giggle.

"What's so funny?" I asked.

"Balt and Kuchoff," he laughed, "I wonder what kind of disturbance they caused."

"Are we really going to go see a Doctor?" I asked.

Brother Fost burst out laughing even more, "Of course not," he chuckled, "What would we tell him?"

"Good point." I agreed.

"I can take care of you just fine until we get to Monere Tower." The priest assured.

The wagon pulled around to the back of 'The Trading Post' and parked.

"Come with me Loher," Zeepha urged, "Let's go in here and get some food for everyone."

"You two stay back here," Loher suggested, "We will be back in a moment."

The sun was high in the sky by the time the wagon carrying Balt, Meeka and Kuchoff arrived at the bridge that separated West Beornan Heafod and East Beornan Heafod.

The conversation was light and cheery as the miles drifted past like leaves floating on a stream.

As they approached the bridge, a few young men jumped out of the trees and grabbed the lead horse in the team, stopping the wagon.

"This is a robbery!" One of the thieves announced.

Several of the thieves were armed with bows and had arrows aimed at Quendonipa.

"What's with the world today?" Kuchoff whispered to Balt.

Balt grabbed his Great Axe and rolled out of the back of the wagon while Meeka began to chant.

Kuchoff took the cue and began to chant a spell of his own.

From under the wagon, Balt counted six young human men about the age of fifteen or sixteen.

Four with bows, one doing the talking and one holding back the team of horses.

"I carry no goods," Quendonipa called, "I sold out yesterday and I'm heading home to get more."

"No goods means a whole lot of gold!" The leader of the group chuckled, "Hand it all over and we won't hurt you."

Balt let out a vicious war cry and rolled out from under the wag-on...in attack mode and ready to fight!

❦

The food was warm and delicious but the chair on which Sir Quinn sat was narrow, uncomfortable and rickety, Sir Quinn could not wait to finish his meal and get up to walk off the cramp he had in his right calf.

"What brings m'lord to Carrington?" The man's wife asked as she served the knight another helping.

"I'm just traveling through," he said, "My home is in Herostun and I intend to make it there as soon as I can."

"What brings you out this far from Herostun?" The man asked.

Sir Quinn thought quickly on his feet, "I applied to be a Royal Soldier for the campaign to that new cave, but I was not accepted."

"That was two months ago," the man countered, "what have you been doing in the meantime?"

"I have a cousin in Steorra," Sir Quinn lied, "I did a bit of visiting."

"It's such a shame about that fire a while back, eh, m'lord?" The woman offered.

"It has been said that they had a little help killin' off what started it." Her husband added.

"Orcs." The knight in disguise confirmed.

"Aye." The woman sighed.

The couple seemed to believe the knight's story and changed the subject.

"Tell me about that girl," the man coaxed.

Again, thinking quickly, the knight answered, "I really don't know, she started following me after I visited the town of Senton."

"Hmm..." The woman thought, "Senton is a nice place, wouldn't you say?"

"If it's all the same to you, Ma'am," Sir Quinn began, "I wouldn't remember, it was night when I stopped in for a meal and a drink and then I left directly after."

"Where are you going after this?" The man asked.

"I'm not quite sure," the knight lied again, "I think I might head back to Salvus Hus, so I don't have to go all the way around past Swapton. I get in trouble if I go into Swapton."

"And why is that, Dearie?" The man's wife asked with a grin.

The knight feigned a laugh and said, "Too many shops and not enough gold."

The couple laughed and smiled at each other.

"That was really a wonderful meal, Ma'am, I thank you," Sir Quinn said as he rose from the table, "I'm sure my horse thanks you as well, Mister."

"It was our pleasure, young man." The wife assured.

"We enjoyed the company." The man announced as he led the knight out to the barn to retrieve his horse.

"And I as well," said the knight.

"If I see her," the man whispered, "I'll tell that girl that you went back to Senton."

"I would appreciate that." Sir Quinn smiled and shook the man's hand.

"You take good care of that horse now, ya hear?" The man said with a wave as Sir Quinn rode off toward the town gates.

"I most certainly will," said the knight, "You can count on that."

Sir Quinn coaxed the white mare into a trot and began to follow the path out of town, gathering speed the further he went until he was at a full gallop.

He headed south toward Swapton and never looked back to see if Angelique was following him.

He hoped the nice man and his wife would stall the vampire hunter long enough for him to get well enough away.

⁕

We slowly ate our meal in the wagon, out of sight, behind the tavern, so enough time would pass and the guards would think that we had in fact, gone to see the local Doctor.

After we figured enough time had gone by and Brother Fost had secretly healed me again without Loher's knowledge so she wouldn't worry, we started out for the gates of town.

As we arrived at the gates of town, one of the guards that had stopped us before stopped us again and asked how I was doing.

Without a word, the guard only had to take one look at me and see that I was apparently doing much better.

"We have the best doctor in Beornan Heafod!" The guard said proudly with his head held high.

"I declare that you do!" Our priest smiled and agreed as the wagon slowly pulled through the gates and headed out of town.

We all sighed a breath of relief as we cleared the town gates and followed the path out of the town toward the bridge that divided the mainland from East Beornan Heafod to West Beornan Heafod.

As we continued on our way, the sun was high in the sky and I was finding it difficult to stay comfortable, it was warmer than I could believe, yet, oddly enough, everyone else was enjoying it.

'I **must** be sick.' I thought silently to myself as I found a cool dark corner and tried to fall asleep.

The ride in the wagon over the rutty dirt path was rough and bouncy, but sleep finally came and I slept like the dead.

Using the blade of his Great Axe as a shield, Balt rushed the closest thief and took them all by surprise.

The commotion frightened the lead horse and made her stand up and forward kick the thief that was holding her, knocking him unconscious to the ground with broken ribs, cuts and bruising.

Two of the four archers fired off a round of arrows, which deflected harmlessly off of the blade of the Great Axe.

The fourth archer ran back into the woods, either afraid, or off to get reinforcements.

Meeka appeared from the inside of the covered wagon and lobbed a few magical ice balls at the fleeing thief, but missed.

Quendonipa quickly rolled back into the covered part of the wagon for shelter and also to grab his sword, he was out in an instant and attacked the leader of the opposing troupe.

Their leader had already engaged his sword and a duel of swords between the two began.

One of the remaining archers suddenly went down to the ground, holding his head and screaming in pain as several of Meeka's ice balls bounced off of his skull.

Balt made easy work of the last remaining archer by squarely punching him directly in the nose and knocking him out.

The duel between the young swordsman and the wagon driver looked like a well-choreographed dance, as blade struck blade and steps were made to evade thrown punches.

Quendonipa smiled at the young man as he sidestepped a thrust and lightly poked him in the rear with the tip of his blade.

The young man winced in pain but still continued to fight.

"Can't you see, boy that I am merely **playing** with you?" Quendonipa chuckled at the young thief, "You're bested, give it up."

"**Never!**" The young man shouted and lunged at him.

"I don't want to kill you." The driver assured as he easily evaded the thrust.

"Good!" The young man shouted in return, "I have no problem with killing you!"

"Yer outnumbered, Boy-o," Balt stated, "If ye kill me friend, I'll 'ave ne choice but te kill ye back."

"I'm not afraid of **you, Dwarf!**" The young man cried as he furiously swung his blade at the wagon driver.

Quendonipa sidestepped the attack with ease and poked the young man in the side, drawing blood this time, "I'm poking you full of holes, boy," the elf said, "Give up while you still can!"

Again, the young man winced out in pain and staggered a bit, "I'll never give up!"

Suddenly, a volley of arrows began to impact the wagon and the surrounding area.

"Take shelter!" Balt ordered as he ducked and rolled out of the arrows' paths.

Meeka grabbed Kuchoff and dove under the wagon as well.

Moments later, in the midst of the sword fight, an uncountable force of young men, dressed in earth-tone attire, wielding swords and bows emerged from the forest from all sides, surrounding the wagon and it's riders.

"Now who's outnumbered, Dwarf?" The young man called out triumphantly.

⁕

By the time Sir Quinn had reached the booming town of Swapton, the sun was directly above his head and he thanked the Gods that he was not wearing his own armor, for it would be absorbing the sun's rays and heating him up.

The knight was fairly sure that the shade of the covered wagon was keeping me cool, as I wore his heavy armor.

These thoughts only ran through his head for a split second and then were gone as he decided to look behind himself to see if he was, in fact, being followed by Angelique, the vampire hunter.

There was no sign of her, but that didn't mean a thing, as sneaky and crafty as she was.

The knight had only hoped that the nice married couple, back in Carrington, had detained the huntress long enough for him to lose her, or better yet, sent her off in the wrong direction, never to be seen again.

The story that he had told the married couple about getting into trouble in Swapton was not exactly untrue, as a boy in his teens, his friends and he would go on long adventures together to explore other towns and areas.

They had made it to Swapton a few times and became tempted by the market and all of the shops within those walls.

A few of his friends had become so tempted, that they had in fact, stolen some goods and got away a few times.

One time, his friends were not so lucky and the guilty parties were caught and punished.

"I'm sure it's not easy trying to live a life with just one hand." He thought to himself, shuddering at the thought.

With these memories now fresh in his mind, the knight decided to bypass Swapton as quickly as he could and go directly to Dournan.

***

"McLaaud," I heard Loher call, "Wake up."

"Our friends are in trouble!" Brother Fost urged, shaking me awake.

As we approached the bridge, we could plainly see the other covered wagon with Meeka and Kuchoff huddled underneath.

Balt was battling half dozen foes and I could not make out who or what they were.

Zeepha gasped as she realized that her husband was in the midst of a sword fight with two others and she began to panic.

Suddenly, Balt was hit by a few arrows and went down to the ground.

I flew into a rage.

Loher suddenly grabbed her own bow and began to fire arrows at the attacking foes as Zeepha urged the team of our horses into a gallop.

Brother Fost began to chant in the halfling tongue as our wagon neared the battlefront.

Upon arrival, Zeepha acquired her own bow and joined Loher in the fight.

Within the cover of arrows, Meeka and Kuchoff began lobbing magical energy bolts at the enemy.

Brother Fost quickly wound his way in an attempt to try to save our fallen dwarven friend while Quendonipa continued to fight for his own life against the two strapping young men.

My own rage was far more than I could control.

Without thinking, I rushed onto the battlefield and began to rip the throats out of the necks of our foes with my bare hands; arrows finding purchase between the plating of Sir Quinn's suit of armor.

I felt nothing.

I walked over to the closest swordsman and picked him up by the throat with one hand; he dropped his sword and struggled within my grasp.

I effortlessly held him there with his feet off the ground, he was gasping for air and his face was turning blue.

With a gagging, gurgling sound, his neck and throat collapsed in my hand as I barely even squeezed.

Quendonipa vanquished the last remaining swordsman, the boy he was fighting before, and then ran to his bride's side.

Behind the wagon, I watched them embrace and kiss and exchange a quick "I love you" in the Elven tongue.

He then took up his own bow and rejoined the fight.

Another arrow found purchase in my left leg and another in my right side.

I ripped the head from the corpse I was holding and swiftly threw it at one of the archers.

The head sailed through the air and found its target on the bridge of the archer's nose.

Upon impact there was a faint cracking sound, immediately followed by a louder crunching sound as the archer's own nose was shattered; spewing blood across his face as well as across the tree he died near.

Two more arrows buried themselves in my back.

I spun around and sprinted at the furthest archer, grabbing up the closest on my way.

With one archer in each hand, I slammed the two bodies together; the end result resembled the worthless remains of a pair of old rag dolls.

I looked over and saw Brother Fost, struggling to drag the wounded Balt to the safety behind one of the wagons.

Dropping the corpse that I held in my hand, I swiftly walked over to the pair of friends, "Save yourself, Brother Fost," I calmly said as another arrow slammed into my side, "I'll carry him to safety."

Brother Fost looked at me with wide, fearful eyes and complied.

He ran to the safety behind one of the wagons as I gathered up my fallen friend and carried him over to join the priest.

Once I felt that all of my friends were safe, I waded back into the sea of arrows, ice balls and energy bolts.

Projectiles whizzed and whirred past my head and arrows impacted my body as I again, stalked each foe, one by one.

If I didn't get a hold on whoever it was that I targeted, the target would panic and run away, just to be pegged off by an arrow or other magical projectile and soon the battle was over; we had won.

There was no cheering.

No glory to be had.

I looked down at my own body and realized that I resembled a feathered porcupine.

Loher couldn't even look at me.

Meeka and Kuchoff just stood and stared in awe and disbelief.

Brother Fost was busy healing our fallen friend Balt and the elven lovers were only interested in each other.

I slowly, painlessly began to pull the arrows that I could reach, out of my own body, dropping them at my feet.

First, Kuchoff walked up and began to help, but he wasn't tall enough to reach them all.

Next was Meeka, who, with each arrow that she removed, winced for me, feeling the pain that just simply wasn't there.

Loher began to search the bodies of the fallen, collecting arrows and blades.

Several of the enemy, although mortally wounded, were still alive and cried out in pain as they lay there, dying.

One by one, Loher put them out of their misery before she searched the corpse.

It was a gruesome sight to behold; it was almost as bad as the slaughter and carnage left behind after an olyame attack, just not as bloody.

Off in the distance, we could hear an approaching rider on horseback.

———◆———

"What have you done to my armor?" Sir Quinn called out in surprise as he rode up to the wagons, "What in Gehenna happened here?"

The armor that I was wearing belonged to the knight, Sir Seth Quinn, my friend, and it was all but ruined.

It was blood stained and full of tiny dents from the impact of hundreds of arrows and rocks.

I looked at the knight, "Well," I said with a smile, "your armor works."

"Look at all of this blood!" Quinn exclaimed.

"I'm afraid that none of it is mine." I commented.

"Well, that's a good thing." The knight smiled and slapped me on the back.

At least a few dozen, if not more bodies laid about the area.

The screams of pain from the not yet dead continued to echo through the air as the sun slowly began to dip down out of sight.

"Balt!" Sir Quinn cried as he noticed, "Is he going to be okay?"

"I'll be foine, Laddie," Balt weakly whispered as we gathered around to see how he was.

"Help me get him up into the wagon," Brother Fost requested, "He'll be fine in a few days, but he needs his rest."

Sir Quinn and I hoisted the dwarven warrior up into the closest wagon and made him as comfortable as possible.

Meeka climbed in with him to keep an eye on his progress.

As I began to walk away, Balt grabbed my arm, "I be in a heap o' appreciation for ye, me guid friend, vampire or no." The dwarf said with a weak smile.

"I don't think that I'm quite yet a vampire, Balt," I smiled, "But not too far from it, I'm afraid."

"Ye cudda fooled me," the dwarf smiled and nodded.

"Get some rest, my friend," I said, "You deserve it."

Sir Quinn tied the white mare to the back of one of the wagons and we all piled in and started toward the town of Dournan.

Brother Fost, Meeka and Kuchoff stayed in the wagon with Balt while Sir Quinn took the reins.

The elven lovers sat up front and took the reins of the second wagon as Loher and I stayed put in the back.

We had decided to get into the safety of Dournan and rest a while before we made any other plans.

It had become quite apparent that I had been infected by the vampire's bite, but we didn't know what stage I was going through, and how far this changing would progress.

I was worried.

So was Loher.

Brother Fost seemed to think that he had the situation well under control, even with Balt being injured.

Only time would tell and the sooner we could get to Monere Tower and seek out Kennis, the better off we would be.

What answers did the old man hold?

Would we ask the correct questions?

So many questions and maybe not enough time...

And where were Brendt and the fairies?

Couldn't **they** do something?

The Circle of Flowers coven...

Giving a willing vampire **back** its soul...

Chapter Three
TRIALS & TRIBULATIONS

What once stood tall as a proud, bustling town, Dournan was now a crumbling ruin of sorrow and despair.

As we entered the town gates, we noticed that there were bodies left lying in the streets, some of which were fresh; most were rotted if not already only bone.

The carnage here was worse than any battlefield I could ever imagine aside from the aftermath against the horrid olyame.

This had very apparently become a lawless town.

Scavengers roamed along, among the ruined buildings, feasting upon the choice pickings, breeding a newer stronger breed of vermin; rats the size of dogs, crows the size of eagles and vultures as big as dwarves and halflings.

Not to mention the foxes, coyotes and wolves.

There were only a few buildings that still stood intact in this town, or what is left of it, namely, the tavern, an armory/weaponry and a few well-built homes, no doubt occupied by unruly unsavory and vile creatures.

"Keep yer wits about ye, Mates," Balt warned as we gathered together outside the tavern.

Sir Quinn and I quickly exchanged our armor once again and it was good to be back in my own fitting clothes; besides, apparently Sir Quinn needed the protection of his own heavy armor more than I.

"Perhaps I should go in first," I suggested, trying to be heard above the commotion and clatter from within the establishment.

"I agree," Sir Quinn stated, "but first, I suggest we get you some sort of chest plate to protect your heart. Losian was well protected while wearing his."

"That armory is still open!" Kuchoff announced as he pointed at the shoppe.

"Come on Balt," the knight coaxed, "let's go in there and get McLaaud a chest plate. I'll make sure it fits me snugly."

"Aye," the dwarf agreed, "ye stay put as te na git inta ne troubles whilst we be gone, Ranger."

"I'll be in the back of one of the wagons," I agreed, "it's too bright and warm out here for me anyway."

Loher shot me one of her quickly becoming famous worried looks as she helped me into the back of the closest wagon.

"Let me heal you again, McLaaud." Brother Fost offered.

"I would rather you didn't," I declined.

"Why not?" Loher asked in shock.

"If he heals me, I may be more vulnerable to any attacks I may receive while in that tavern. We need all of the protection we can get right now."

"I'm sorry, Loher," Meeka added, "I feel the need to agree with him on this one."

"As much as it's against my better judgment, I will honor your request for now," the priest submitted.

Loher stood silent for a moment and then asked, "Why are we even going into that tavern?"

"To gain some well needed information about the Tower and what lies between here and there," I answered, a bit more sternly than I had intended.

Loher frowned and looked away, "Well, I'm not going to go in there and watch you get hurt. Kuchoff, Meeka and I are staying right here."

Before any of the others could say a word, Brother Fost piped up and announced, "And I'm staying out here as well."

"Good," I agreed, "You'll all probably just get in the way!" I uncontrollably growled as I turned away into the shadows.

"What in Gehenna's name was **that** all about?" I heard Sir Quinn ask as he and Balt returned with my new chest plate.

"We all have decided to remain out here while the three of you go into the tavern," Brother Fost explained.

"I never agreed to such a thing," Kuchoff countered.

"I'm going in **alone!**" I snapped as I snatched the chest plate away from the knight.

Surprised at the sudden action, Sir Quinn took a quick step back and counted his fingers to see if I had taken any off, "What's with him?"

"The necromorphosis is taking over," Brother Fost expounded.

"Necro-what?" several of my companions echoed.

"Necromorphosis is the condition our dear friend is going through right now, due to the bite he received from the vampire. It's the transformation from being alive to being undead." Brother Fost explained. "His body is slowly dying, but will continue to function; in fact, his senses are becoming more acute, and he is becoming physically stronger. The only down-side to this transformation is that his mind and attitude are becoming more animalistic in nature and he will cease to act or think like a civilized half-elf."

"Has he ever been civilized?" The knight joked.

"You're acting like I'm not even here!" I growled and quickly bolted out of the wagon at them.

I got within a few inches of grabbing Sir Quinn's throat, but then stopped.

A Holy Bolt from Brother Fost's Blessed Crossbow bounced off of the new chest plate armor that I had hidden beneath my tunic.

I was only joking, McLaaud." The knight spat.

I laughed, half ignoring his words, "Well, I guess that was a successful test."

"A test of **what**, exactly?" The knight asked with a waiver of mixed fear and anger in his voice.

"To see if the chest plate would work," Kuchoff answered.

I smiled.

"We also know that Brother Fost is ready and willing to destroy you as well," Meeka added, barely shaken, "It all happened so quickly!"

I smiled again.

"T'is guid te see tat ye still 'ave some self-control, Mate," Balt observed.

"I want you all to know that I will never do anything to harm any of you," I announced, "Brother Fost is right, I **am** changing and my personality may not be as... civilized as it used to be, but I still have this team's best interests in mind. Besides, I don't **want** to turn into a vampire, so the sooner we find out where Kennis is, and how to get there, the sooner we can learn how to change me back."

Suddenly there was a loud crash and some yelling coming from within the tavern, drawing our attention back to the task at hand.

"Are ye ready, Mate?" the dwarven fighter asked.

"I'm going in alone," I calmly repeated.

"Be careful in there," Loher pleaded as I began to walk toward the tavern door.

I turned around to face her and simply smiled and patted the chest plate where the Holy Bolt had bounced off.

Loher forced a smile and nodded her understanding.

I turned again and entered the tavern... alone.

I stood in the entrance of the tavern, expecting to have to let my eyes adjust to the sudden dimness of the windowless room, and surprisingly, it didn't take that long at all.

The tavern was filled with mostly men.

Gruff, unclean and obnoxious.

They were pushing a young orc around, from man to man, teasing it, taunting it, shoving it into the walls and pushing it over tables and chairs.

The orc was helpless, badly beaten, unarmed, overpowered and outnumbered.

In the commotion, no one even noticed me enter, so, walking past overturned tables and stepping over broken chairs, I calmly strolled to the bar as slowly as I could, as to not raise any suspicions of my vampiric speed.

I got the attention of the barkeep and ordered ale.

The young orc was pushed into the bar about an arm's reach away from me; I did not interfere.

The drink was served and upon paying for it, I leaned forward and asked if the Barkeep knew of Kennis.

He shook his head 'No,' but pointed to a solitary figure sitting at a table near the door.

Without hesitation, but still keeping my speed down to a minimum, I made my way over to strike up a conversation.

A large human male picked the young orc up by its feet, upending it, its head bouncing off the floor; the man violently tossed the creature to another group of men.

Laughter erupted as the men purposely missed catching the orc and let it slam into a table, splintering it in two.

The orc scrambled to his feet and began to run for the door, only to be stopped by yet another group of men entering the tavern.

Their leader swiftly scooped up the young orc and heaved him back into the waiting crowd.

The game began again.

I was becoming glad that my companions had not insisted on joining me.

Each and every one, except perhaps Balt would have been upset at the goings on in here.

"Excuse me," I said, standing before the hooded figure that sat there.

There was no response.

"I was wondering if I could ask you a few questions," I tried again.

There was still no movement from the hooded figure.

A loud crack and the sound of shattering glass attempted to steal my attention, but I stood steady, still staring at the mysterious hooded figure.

I pulled out a gold coin and tossed it on the table in front of the figure, it landed and spun for a moment and then finally settled with a slight chime.

Without looking up, the figure placed a gloved hand over the coin and slid it from the table, into safekeeping.

Another loud crash, this time, directly behind me as the young orc was body slammed into a table; wood splintered across the room.

I sat down across from the figure and took a pull from my ale, it tasted pungent and foul.

"Ask," the figure hissed raucously.

"What do you know of Kennis?" I asked.

The figure slowly raised its head, and I could scarcely make out the features of an aged, creased, humanoid face, "Kennis..." the figure echoed, drawing out the 's' sound.

"That's right," I answered, "and Monere Tower."

"If you make it to the tower, you'll find him there," the figure rasped, lowering its head.

"What lies between here and the tower?" I prodded.

The figure said nothing.

The men howled out with laughter as the young orc attempted to fight back.

I rolled another coin across the table.

The figure scooped the coin from the table and slowly looked up again, "The Charon Swamp lies between here and there. Find the path."

I rolled one more coin to the figure and asked, "Once inside the tower, what shall be expected?"

"**Death!**" the figure laughed loudly and then vomited live spiders and other various insects across the table in my direction; I watched them scatter away into the dark corners and down into cracks in the floor.

When I finally looked up once again, the figure was gone.

The orc lay dead on the floor.

I rose to my feet and started for the exit.

"Hey stranger," one of the men called to me, "would you mind dragging that filth outta here..."

Without turning or even acknowledging him, I left and closed the door, cutting him off in mid-sentence.

The sun was reaching its lowest point in the sky, just before setting, yet it was still a bit too bright for my own taste; I went immediately into the cover of one of the wagons.

"Well, he's still in one piece and not covered in blood, so I'm assuming that it went well and he has some answers," Meeka observed aloud to our companions.

"Should we go ask him?" Kuchoff asked.

"Perhaps we should wait for him to come tell us," Sir Quinn suggested.

"I'll go," Loher offered.

"I'll be goin' wit ye, Lass," Balt added.

As I was climbing out of the wagon, Quendonipa and Zeepha had finished transferring all of our personal effects and mounts to one wagon (the wagon that I was in) and announced that they were going to take the second wagon and return back to Salvus Hus by taking the long way around, just in case they were to be spotted by the vampire hunter, Angelique DeStruere.

We agreed and bid them both farewell, thanking them for all that they had done.

"Thank Festus for us as well," I offered as the pair of elves pulled away and headed for the ruined gates of town.

"We will," Zeepha promised, and the wagon disappeared into the night.

"So, McLaaud, did you get any answers?" Sir Quinn queried.

"Answers I have, as well as an uncontrollable hunger," I admitted, "Is anyone up for a bit of gratuitous violence?"

"What do you mean?" Brother Fost asked in surprise.

"I'm hungry," I reiterated, "I'm going back in there to feed."

"Let me heal you!" Brother Fost pleaded, "We are unsure what will happen if you feed!"

"I know exactly what will happen if I feed, **I won't be hungry!**" I howled, "Heal me if you must, but if it doesn't help, I'm going back in there to **feed**, and I want at least Balt to go in with me to cover my back!"

"I'll na be killin' fer no reason, Elf," Balt instructed, "but cover yer back I'll do."

"The same goes for me," Sir Quinn added, "I'll back you up though, if you need it."

"Just make sure that they're all dead," Meeka warned, "We don't need any **more** vampires coming after us."

"I'll second that," Loher agreed.

"Heal me Fost," I urged, "quickly, I'm **starving!**"

"Sit down here," Brother Fost said, pointing to a broken piece of stone wall, "I'm going to use just about every ounce of power I can muster, just so you don't **have to** kill unnecessarily."

"Believe me, Brother," I cooed, "I don't **want** to kill anyone, but if I don't take care of this hunger…"

"Hush now, McLaaud," Brother Fost scolded, "I'm concentrating."

The night sky was closing in on us quickly as Brother Fost summoned up all of the powers of his God, Onh.

He prayed his words over me as he laid his hands upon my flesh, and just as the sun completely dipped down below the horizon, I felt a sudden shock to my soul and the hunger went away.

Tears filled my eyes and sudden warmth filled my body.

I felt alive again.

Alive, but weak.

"How do you feel, McLaaud?" The priest asked.

"I **feel** again," I stuttered, "it worked! The hunger is gone!"

"Quickly," Sir Quinn gasped, "into the wagon!"

We could see the shadows bringing forth the new breeds of vermin, hunting out their own meals of the night.

"This place was not safe to begin with, friends," Kuchoff announced, "it has just become even more unsafe!"

We all piled into the wagon with Sir Quinn at the reigns.

"Let's get out of here!" Meeka cried.

"Where to?" Sir Quinn asked.

"Head south," I answered, "to the Charon Swamp."

"I know of a monastery near that swamp," Brother Fost gleefully announced, "I'll lead you there once we get close."

"Will they give us any help?" Sir Quinn asked.

"Of course they will, my son," Brother Fost quipped, "they're priests, like me!"

"What if they learn of McLaaud's condition?" Loher asked, suddenly in a panic.

"I'm counting on it, my dear," the priest soothed, "They may be able to collectively heal him for good."

"Then we won't have to go into the swamp to find the tower." I reckoned.

"And this whole nightmare will be done?" Meeka hoped.

"Na quite, Lassie," Balt countered, "tat twit Angelique is still out tere somewheres, an she'll still be lookin' fer us all ta same."

"But if she sees that he's been healed," Meeka began to argue.

"She may na give 'im ta chance ta show 'er," Balt cut her off.

"Then we'll just have to fight her," Kuchoff angrily added, pounding his fist into his own cupped hand.

"Now ye be talkin' Boy-o!" Balt proudly laughed and reached over to playfully muss the young Psionisist's hair.

After a few hours of riding and idle chatter, Sir Quinn announced, "I'm not sure about the rest of you, but I'm beginning to get a bit hungry. I suggest we stop and set up camp, we're far enough away from Dournan, so we should be quite safe."

"Keep yer eyes open," Balt warned, "can't ever be too sure tat we're safe."

The camp was set up and run as usual, Balt took care of the weapons and armor in case they had at all become damaged or dirty and this time they all needed some love and care.

Loher and I went out hunting.

Meeka and Sir Quinn took care of the mounts.

Brother Fost set the fire and began preparation for the meal, while Kuchoff set up a Psionic field around the perimeter of our camp to insure added safety.

Hunting in the swamp was not exactly the easiest thing to do, because for one, some of the creatures there are far more dangerous than most of the foes that we have encountered.

For two, they were very well hidden from our elven infrared vision due to the clay-like mud that covered their cold-blooded bodies, blocking almost any source of heat emanating through.

The third and final reason was, that neither of us was used to the swamp like conditions; the footing was unstable, our movements were slow and we weren't as agile as we were used to being.

I also had lost my newly acquired vampiric speed since Brother Fost had healed me.

After what seemed like hours, we lucked out and bagged a few coypu, which are large destructive rodents that feed mainly on the vegetation found under the surface of the water.

We returned to the camp and Balt immediately demanded that we turn our boots over to him for cleaning and repair.

Brother Fost joyfully snatched up the meat and began cooking it as Loher and I warmed our dampened feet by the fire.

Kuchoff surprised us all with a delicious handpicked green salad and had also discovered a flask of wine in the back of the wagon; it went very well with the sweet and tender coypu meat.

Regardless of the dismal surroundings of the swamp and all of the insects that came with it, we had a fairly good time that night.

The meal was good and filling, the conversation had never gone stale and we were never ambushed or even remotely attacked in any way, other than the almost bird sized mosquitoes.

⚬

After a few hours of rest or sleep, the morning sun had begun to rise as we packed up the wagon and headed for the monastery that Brother Fost had spoken of.

"Keep your eyes open for some sort of a path that leads through the center of this swamp," I urged, "just in case we need it."

"Knowin' our luck," Balt began, "we prolly will."

"I don't even **see** a tower," Meeka commented.

"All **I** see is fog," Kuchoff added in agreement.

"How much further to your friends?" Sir Quinn asked the priest.

"We are being guided by a higher power, my son," Brother Fost murmured with a smile, "patience is a virtue."

"Is it just me," Kuchoff chuckled, "or is Brother Fost becoming increasingly 'holy' lately?"

"What do you mean?" Meeka asked.

"The whole 'My son' thing," Kuchoff replied, "he never said that before."

"We were never keeping the company of a pseudo-vampire before," Brother Fost justified.

The day had become bright and sunny, and my companions were enjoying the warmth.

I, however, was miserable as the Necromorphosis slowly began to regain control of my thoughts and actions.

"I hope we are near enough to the monastery, Brother Fost," I said as I shrunk down into the shadow in the corner of the wagon.

"Is it happening again?" The priest asked.

"Indeed," I answered.

"We will be there shortly," he assured me, "Quicken the pace, good Sir Knight," He called to Sir Quinn up front.

Sir Quinn just nodded and snapped the reigns to speed up the horses.

A small copse of trees could be seen not too far ahead of us, growing larger as the distance between shortened.

"There," the priest said, pointing to the grouping, "head for those trees."

Sir Quinn pulled the reigns to one side and the mounts obeyed, turning slightly to the right to head straight for the ever-growing grove.

A large stone structure could be seen now, resting in the center of the grove of various fruit bearing trees.

Birds of all colors and sizes flocked on or near the trees, feeding on the wealth of nourishment found there.

"Where were those birds when we needed them last night?" Meeka rhetorically asked.

As we traveled further down the path, several monks in brown robes could be seen tending gardens and free roaming livestock.

As we entered the clearing near the structure, we were met by a middle aged man dressed in an out-dated Royal Soldier's uniform and three hooded monks, their hands and arms held out in gestures of welcome and acceptance.

We pulled up to our greeters and stopped the wagon, the monks bowed their heads and the man stepped closer, "Welcome travelers, welcome to Inundo Abbey, are you in need of any assistance?" The man asked as he placed his hand on the nose of our lead horse.

The horse nickered quietly and nuzzled his hand.

Sir Quinn jumped down from the wagon, "I am Sir Seth Quinn of Salvus Hus," he bowed low, "my companions are few but varied, two of which are in need of assistance."

As the knight spoke, Loher and Meeka helped Balt to the ground and then assisted me.

"Good Sir Knight," the man exclaimed, "we are honored to be of any assistance."

Two of the monks then stepped forward and assisted Balt to the main door of the monastery as the man and Sir Quinn helped me.

Brother Fost was quick on our heels.

"Your dwarven friend has seen a bit of action, I can see, but pray tell, what is ailing the Elf?" The man asked as we entered the oratory.

"Half-elf," I corrected weakly.

"I apologize for my mistake my Lord," the man submitted.

"I healed the dwarf as best as I could," Brother Fost offered, "and the half-elf is suffering from an infection of the blood."

The infirmary is this way," the man announced as he quickly led us all down a narrow hallway.

Unlike the castle in Salvus Hus, which has great halls of marble, the halls here were narrow and built modestly of fieldstone and crude mud mortar.

Upkeep to the structural integrity was a welcomed and very necessary daily task for the monks.

As we zigged and zagged through the narrow hallways of the monastery, we passed a large refectory and several small dorms.

After a while, we passed a fairly large balneary and then finally arrived at the infirmary.

The monks assisted Balt to a crudely made straw bed as I was laid down on a similar one.

"Rest now, McLaaud," Brother Fost assured, "we are safe here."

"That is good advice, Brother..." the man coaxed.

"Fost," the priest answered, "Brother Fost Atlberry of Hydan Seir, disciple of Onh."

The man chuckled and averted his eyes, "I am but a wayward soul whose name is unimportant, trying to make peace with my past by helping the monks here in the Abbey."

"You're an outlaw?" Kuchoff guessed.

"**Kuchoff!!**" Meeka scolded.

"Unfortunately, your son is correct, my Lady," the outlaw admitted, "but as long as I stay within these sacred walls, the old Tyrant King cannot touch me."

"Out of curiosity," Loher replied, "how long have you been here?"

The outlaw laughed again, "More years than I care to count, my Lady, I lost track after fifteen."

Sir Quinn smiled, "I'm afraid that I must be the bearer of some unpleasant news..."

"Pray tell, good Sir Knight," the outlaw wheedled.

"The old King is dead and his very young son, Lagu Ofer'Eal, has claimed the throne; a good three years now, or more," Sir Quinn conferred.

The outlaw snorted jovially, "Then I'm free? Why would that be unpleasant?"

"It looks that way," Brother Fost grinned, "it would be unpleasant to know now that you have been here for three years too long. Your name dear Sir?"

The outlaw stopped grinning and straightened his posture, "How do I know that this isn't a trick?"

"I am a Priest of Onh, and he is a knight; both sworn to honesty," Brother Fost retorted.

"So, there really **is** a new King?" The man asked.

"On my word of honor, there is," the knight confirmed.

The man hesitated and dropped off into deep thought for a moment and then finally announced, "Byron Le'Abboltt, at your service."

Sir Quinn gasped, "Not **the** Byron Le'Abboltt that was once the fiercest Royal Soldier that Beornan Heafod has ever seen?"

Byron chuckled again, "Well, I wouldn't go as far as to say the fiercest, but yes, I was once a Royal Soldier."

"That explains the outdated soldier's uniform." The knight conveyed.

Two monks entered the room and surveyed the scene, one went to where Balt was laying and the other came to me.

"The dwarf's wounds have already been healed, he probably needs only rest and proper nourishment," Byron explained to Balt's caregiver, "this one," he said, indicating me, "is suffering from Necromorphosis due to a vampire bite."

Brother Fost was taken aback, "How did you know?"

"I saw the bite mark scars when we brought him in and laid him down on the cot," Byron admitted.

"I healed him the best I could, but only succeeded in slowing down the process," the halfling divulged.

"We were on our way to find Kennis in Monere Tower when we were attacked by a group of thieves," Sir Quinn explained, "hence, Balt's wounds."

"The Monere Tower?" Byron questioned, "You'll find more than just Kennis there, heed my warning!"

"We are aware of the warnings," Sir Quinn remarked.

"We were wondering if there might be a possibility that a large group of monks would be able to collectively heal him, permanently curing him of the Necromorphosis, so we don't **have to** go find Kennis," Brother Fost added.

"I have never heard of such a thing," Byron admitted, "but it might be worth a try."

Suddenly, from off within the inner chambers of the oratory, a gong sounded.

⸻⸺◆⸺⸻

"Meal time," Byron announced, "time for you all to get some proper nourishment into your bodies and then some rest, and you all need it."

We were escorted by Byron and the monks, back to the refectory.

The refectory was a long room with glazed windows on both of the long walls.

There were long plain tables standing in two rows in the center of the room; the seats were hard and unpadded.

Hundreds of monks filed slowly into the room and sat at the tables as various raced children ranging from the ages of five through twelve quietly served the monks their meals in crude wooden bowls.

Byron, my companions and I were sat at a smaller table off to the side of the room our voices were kept down to a minimum as most of the conversation was communicated through unexplained hand gestures that my companions and I could not understand.

The refectory was vast and silent as the monks ate what looked like a plain porridge-like substance.

My companions seated at the smaller table were served pheasant and fruit, while I was served an underdone slab of some kind of unidentifiable red meat and a mug of an also unidentifiable herbal/protein concoction; both looked hideous but the flavor of it all was most pleasing.

◄○►

After the meal, Balt and I were escorted back to the infirmary, while the rest of our friends were shown to their dormitories for the night.

Loher had wanted to stay with me, but Byron insisted that she stay in her room with Meeka; she reluctantly complied.

Within an hour, I could hear Balt, snoring away in dreamland; I was uncomfortably restless due to the fact that I was becoming nocturnal in nature.

Two of the monks were posted to guard the door of the infirmary.

The only reason for the guards that I could figure, was that they saw me as a plausible threat and wanted the extra protection; not that they would have done any good against me, or any other vampire for that matter, but they felt protected all the same.

There must have been something to that herbal/protein drink that I was served because I fell into a peaceful, restful sleep and actually dreamt of good things from my past; it has been quite a while since that has happened.

Not since those damn olyame.

I dreamt of long ago, when I was a young child, the day my father presented me with a young colt for my own.

I named him Stahvee, which was a word I had heard my elders use to describe a rare and beautiful object.

❧

I was awoken by a heavy feeling on my arms, chest and legs and I could not move my head.

I opened my eyes to find an uncountable number of monks, headed by Brother Fost, laying their hands upon me and praying in various tongues.

The chorus was massively confusing and frightening to say the least and the pain that followed was undeniably intense.

Shockwaves of hot and cold ripped through my body, convincing me that I was encased in a block of ice while being bathed in a blanket of lightning.

I tried to scream, but my teeth were clamped down tightly on some sort of wooden dowel to stop me from clenching my teeth or biting off my own tongue. My voice just squeaked out, as I could barely breathe due to the constriction of the monks pressing down on me.

Sweat oozed out of every pore of my body and tears filled my eyes and streamed down my face; I was not ready for any of this.

I uncontrollably lost my bowels as well as urinated all over myself, but the monks paid no mind and continued their task.

With every new verse of the various chants, a wave of what felt like lightning once again, passed through me, greatly intensifying with each passing breath.

Hot then cold...

Burning then freezing...

Trying to draw a breath...

It was just too much.

I finally blacked out once again.

⸻

I awoke once some time later with Balt sitting on the edge of my cot.

"Tat was some nightmare, eh McLaaud?" The dwarf chuckled.

As I tried to sit up, my back sang out with snaps, pops and creaks.

I quickly examined myself to see if I was still stewing in my own urine and excrement, but alas, no; I had been bathed and changed into clean clothing.

I felt relieved.

The warrior braced my shoulders with his hands and propped up the crude pillow behind me, allowing me to semi-comfortably settle back in a slight sitting position.

"Did it work?" I asked my friend.

"Tat remains ta be seen, Elf," he presumed.

"How long was I asleep?"

"Long 'nuff tat I be tinkin' ye died."

"How do I look?"

"Like ye been chewed up an' spit out, how d'ya feel?"

"Like I've been chewed up and left for excrement," I tried to smile.

The dwarf did a fine enough job smiling for the both of us as his grin went from ear to ear and shone brightly beneath the thick reddish calico beard that all but covered the lower portion of his face, "T'least ye donna smell like it no more."

He let out a hearty laugh that shook dust from the walls and drew the attention of our friends who suddenly came rushing in.

"Give him air!" Brother Fost commanded as the group surrounded me, "Don't crowd him!"

My excited companions backed off slightly, launching questions at me as if I...

"You all act like I was raised from the dead!" I exclaimed.

The questions stopped and the room fell silent; the smiling faces all turned grim within the blink of an eye.

"You were, McLaaud," Loher half whispered as if even she didn't want to hear what she had to say, "your heart stopped beating and your lips turned dark blue."

"Aye, Mate," Balt agreed, "I telled ya tat I tought ye be dead."

"Your skin was ice cold and you weren't breathing." Meeka sniffled.

"We thought we had lost you." Kuchoff added with his usual toothy grin.

I noticed that Sir Quinn and Byron were nowhere to be seen, but as usual, as if right on cue, "Well... you look strong enough to take on a dozen orcs single handed!" Sir Quinn chimed as he entered the room, "That is, if they were all drunk and passed out asleep," he laughed.

The knight strode over and lightly slapped my back as a greeting.

I weakly smiled and tried to get up.

"You need your rest if we're going to go to Monere Tower," Byron announced as he too, entered the room.

"The Tower?" I asked confused, "The healing didn't work?" "I'm afraid not my son," Brother Fost responded sorrowfully.

"But..." I began.

"What the monks and I did to you will only assure that the Necromorphosis can be controlled to a certain extent," the priest explained, "so think of that control as a temporary gift. A gift that is still slowly killing you if we don't get to Kennis and find out how to stop it."

"And the good news is," Byron piped in, "that I will personally guide you to, through and back from the Tower, as I have been there a few times before within the past few years. It's a great place to hide from bounty-hunters."

"So rest easy now my friend," Sir Quinn mock ordered, "we have a precarious journey ahead of us as soon as you're able."

"How long until the Necromorphosis becomes unstable again, Brother Fost?" I inquired.

"I have no answer for that," the priest confessed, "get some rest so we can depart soon."

My companions slowly exited the infirmary, including Balt; Loher deeply kissed me before she turned and followed the rest out.

I settled back into a comfortable position and quickly drifted back into a deep, deep sleep.

Dreams of my father, The Seolfer Wudu and Stahvee filled the void between dreams of Loher, the cave and The Scorpion.

⸻ ❖ ⸻

Hours must have passed as I was awakened by the sound of the gong.

My stomach was growling loudly from an intense hunger, like I had not eaten in days.

(Perhaps I hadn't.)

A monk entered the room and helped me from the cot, and as he attempted to help me, I noticed that my strength had returned and I needed no help.

Standing, I suddenly realized that it seemed as if I was almost weightless and that my vampiric speed had returned, yet I **felt** like I did before I was bitten.

The monk silently escorted me to the refectory and seated me with my friends.

The usual meals of porridge for the monks and the red meat and weird liquid mixture for me were served to us by a young dwarven girl, but this time it was an odd fishy smelling soup for my friends, which must not have been too entirely bad, because they finished every last bite.

I'm guessing it was some kind of turtle, or perhaps alligator or snake.

The meal was completed without a single word and we were led outside.

The sun was low in the sky and gaining altitude and I noticed that neither the sunlight nor the warm start of summer heat affected me like it once did before.

Chapter Four

INSTABILITY

Byron Le'Abboltt definitely knew his way around in the Charon Swamp as he led the team down a secret hidden path right to the natural path that went through the center.

This must be the path in the center that the cloaked horror had spoken of in the tavern in Dournan.

Byron must have created this secret path not long after arriving at the Abby so many years ago in order to have an escape route from the bounty hunters that were charged to find and return him to the old Tyrannical King.

Dead or alive.

Surprisingly, the path wasn't all that far away from the entrance to the Abbey itself.

How had we missed it?

The path stretched through the swampland, twisting and turning, passing through shallow, ankle deep muck and saw grass that would cut flesh as easily as a well-honed blade fresh from the whetstone.

"There is a stable dry spot a little way in," Byron explained, "I suggest we get there before nightfall and set up camp. It's too dangerous to try to make it through at night.

Less than an hour later, the team arrived at the dry spot and began to set up camp.

Everyone did their usual part while Byron collected scarce firewood.

As the sun dipped down toward the horizon and the fire glowed a bit stronger, it began casting dancing shadows across the distant trees.

Kuchoff began to reflect on the events of recent past...

"Byron," Kuchoff prompted, "Who were all of those children there at the monastery?"

"Orphans," he answered.

Kuchoff turned to gaze at Meeka as she tended the fire, unaware of the boy's stare.

The Psionisist began to smile his infamous toothy grin, "She's not really my mother," Kuchoff confessed, "my parents were killed by hobgoblins and Meeka accepted me as hers."

"Well, my boy," Byron chuckled, "it seems as though this whole team has accepted you."

"I could have become one of those orphans," Kuchoff remarked as he lost his grin.

"There are far worse places to be than an orphanage," Byron consoled.

"Like where?" The boy asked.

"Monere Tower," the veteran soldier whispered and then turned away into the shadows.

The boy sat there for a moment, thinking about what had just transpired and then got up and moved closer to Meeka.

"Are you alright?" she asked as he sat down next to her.

"I'm fine," he assured her and tossed a small stick into the fire, raising bright orange sparks that danced in the breeze and then finally faded away.

We sat, talking and telling stories of our respective pasts as the sun completely disappeared below the horizon.

We learned little of Byron's past as he mostly sat silently, paying attention to whatever was dancing around through his own mind.

An owl hooted along with the chorus of peeper frogs, seemingly keeping time with the amphibious chants while a whippoorwill brought up the rhythm, creating a natural nocturnal symphony.

The night sky was filled with familiar stars and a swollen full moon that somehow reminded me of the night that we first met Losian Sawol, although it was just a faint sliver of the moon that night.

(["Shouldn't we have a full moon for an occasion such as this?" I quipped, trying to lessen my own fear.

The vampire's smile widened and it let out a ghoulish laugh; apparently, it, but no one else thought what I had said was funny.])

Losian's laugh still haunted my memory, its laugh, those eyes, and... rats!

(["Don't look at its eyes!" The priest called out as a warning, "Do not look it in the eyes!" He repeated and continued to call out to us.

Quickly, I lowered my gaze and noticed a few hundred rats moving about the vampire's feet, creating the odd effect of a shadow; the rats pooled around it like some sort of large carpet of flesh and fur.])

(Rats!!!)

Slowly, I looked down at my feet and noticed a half dozen large black rats casually strolling about my feet as if they belonged there.

I kicked one away, but it just shook off the disturbance and returned back to where it had once been perched atop my boot.

I kicked it off again and stomped on it; the others scurried away in fear.

"What are you doing, McLaaud?" Loher asked, getting up and walking toward me.

I secretly kicked the dead rat into the brush before she was near enough to notice, "Knocking muck off of my boots," I half lied.

The elven maiden gently took a hold of my hand, "Come sit by me," she entreated.

I followed her to the fire, where Balt was showing Sir Quinn an old dwarven trick on how to silently smooth out damaged armor without the use of a hammer.

"Na juss any stane'll work, it's gotta be a smooth'n like tis'n," the dwarf tried to explain, but the knight just looked confused.

"Let me translate for you, Sir Quinn," Brother Fost laughed. "He said, 'Not just any stone will work, it's got to be a smooth one, like this one.' Please continue, Balt."

"Verra guid," Balt agreed. "Ye do ta translatin' an' I'll do ta explain-in'."

"This is quite interesting," Brother Fost admitted with a chuckle.

Byron moved closer to the fire to watch as well; it was as if we were all becoming a growing happy family once again.

"Ye heat up ta spot on ta armor wot ye wanna smooth out," Balt began.

"I understood that bit," the knight stated.

The rest of us agreed.

"Donna heat it up te much 'er ye'll warp it."

This time it was Byron that looked confused.

"Don't heat it up too much or you'll warp it," Sir Quinn translated.

"Ahh, I see," Byron nodded.

"It takes a while to understand our dear dwarven friend," Meeka giggled.

"Sum longer tan udders," Balt playfully jeered at the knight.

Meeka giggled again, this time joined by Kuchoff.

"Once ye gots it heated enuff," Balt continued, "ye puts it on sum leather and roll yer stane across the dent, like tiss."

The dwarf rolled the smooth stone over the dented armor, putting almost all of his weight in on the action; there was a muffled pop and the dent went away.

"Amazing!" Sir Quinn gasped.

"Ye lets it cool off a bit, an' then go on te ta next'n."

"Good as new," Kuchoff smiled.

"Almose," Balt uttered, "na as strong anymore, but almose."

"I hate to spoil the fun," Meeka announced as she rose to her feet, mussing Kuchoff's hair on her way up, "but it's getting late and **we** are going to sleep."

Kuchoff's smile quickly turned to a frown.

"Did you set the Psi web around the camp?" Meeka asked the boy.

"As soon as we got here," Kuchoff smiled again.

"Psi web?" Byron asked.

"I'm a Psionisist," Kuchoff stated.

"I'm not sure that I know what you mean," Byron confessed.

Ironically, as if on cue, a small portion of the Psionic web around the camp suddenly sizzled.

"I'll show you," Kuchoff grinned, and began to prance proudly toward where the sound was made. "I can create a protective border around our camp, to keep the nasties out." "So it's magic?" Byron asked.

"No," the boy giggled, "It's too confusing to explain," Kuchoff said, looking for what caused the noise, "it's easier to **think** of it as a sort of magic, so, yes, but not really."

Byron, Kuchoff and Meeka searched the area for whatever creature it was that sizzled against the web.

"Here it is," Meeka announced, holding up a very large, still smoldering rat.

Byron examined the rat, "A common field rat?" He rhetorically asked, "What is a field rat doing so close to the swamps?"

"It's dead now," Kuchoff shrugged and scampered back to the fire, Meeka followed soon after.

Byron also shrugged it off and returned to the fire as well.

(Rats!!!)

I stood there, barely breathing, wondering how long it was going to take them to figure out that, the rats 'belonged' to me.

⸻◆⸻

After Meeka and Kuchoff retired to their tent, one by one, the rest of the party followed behind and retired as well...

...Everyone except Loher.

She kept on staring at me with a worried look in her eyes.

I tried to convince her to relax and that I would be fine; she would agree, but that worried look never left her face, nor would her eyes cease their gaze upon me.

Finally, the events of the past day must have gotten the better of her because her head began to nod and her eyes slipped down, lowering her steady gaze.

Her reverie had begun.

Moving quickly and quietly, I dashed away from the fire and out of the camp, careful not to disturb Kuchoff's Psionic web.

My hunger had grown to new heights.

"Byron's warning of dangerous creatures had better not be over exaggerated." I thought to myself as I searched for my next meal.

Once I was sure I was far enough away from camp so I couldn't be heard by even Loher's ears, I decided I could afford to make noise.

I purposely stepped down hard on a twig to make it snap... Nothing.

I bounced around from tree to tree, shaking them as I went... Nothing.

I picked up an old rotting stump and tossed it... Nothing.

Nothing seemed to work and I was becoming angry at Byron's over exaggeration of the supposed dangers of this swamp.

I had, however noticed that I had seen some fresh, rather large feline prints in the shallow muck near the stump I had dug up.

"Here kitty, kitty, kitty," I called; my voice was more of a growl than my own voice.

I searched for almost an hour, but came up short.

Just as I was about to turn and head hungry back to camp, I heard a low growl to my left.

Smiling and swallowing back saliva from my watering mouth, I spun to the left and lurched forward.

My hands plunged into the soft thick fur of the poised to pounce cougar that had apparently been stalking me.

Without even thinking, my mouth opened wide as my body contorted around to aim my face at the jugular vein in the creature's throat.

Simultaneously, my fingers and teeth clamped down around my victim's neck.

Warm rivulets of thick nourishing blood oozed down my throat as the mighty heart of the beast sped up from terror; I could feel it beating through my fingertips.

The beast was still alive and struggling as I got my fill from the blood.

Instinctually, (apparently) my body once again contorted around the cougar, my fingers still firmly grasping the creature's neck.

There was a gurgling snap and the beast lay bleeding at my feet. Dead.

Satisfied, I slowly began my walk back to the camp.

I was still awake as Loher came out of her reverie and the others began to wake up.

The sun was just about to crack over the horizon and shine over the still sleeping world.

I was just about to load the last of our camping supplies into the wagon when the first rays of sunshine landed on my skin; the extreme warmth was almost painful, but it did no damage... yet.

I quickly moved into the still shaded shadow of the wagon and tried to act as natural as possible.

It was a good thing my companions were still half asleep and not paying too much attention to me.

"Who's up for some breakfast?" Brother Fost asked aloud as he fished out some dried meat and fruits from a pack.

Kuchoff, Meeka and Sir Quinn gathered around the priest and received large handfuls of the food.

Although I had secretly fed on the blood of a cougar while my companions were otherwise engaged in rest, I decided to take a small portion of the dried meat anyway, as to not arouse any suspicions.

"I suggest that when you are done with your meal, we get back on the path," Byron announced, "Daylight doesn't make it any less dangerous in the Charon Swamp."

At that, I had to laugh.

We finished our meal, covered the remains of the fire and packed up the rest of our supplies.

By the time we continued on the path to the tower, the sun was above the horizon and I had to keep within the shadows of the wagon's interior.

I was soon asleep, covered by an extra wagon cover to keep the sun away.

My companions must have gotten used to the fact that I was always staying out of the sun now, as they rarely, if ever spoke of it.

I was awoken by the wagon stopping abruptly, accompanied by yelling and cursing.

I poked my head out from beneath my cover to notice that the sun was now high in the sky and I was alone in the back.

The sounds of a skirmish reached my ears along with the angry voices.

Inhuman screams of pain, the clashing of metal on metal and the all too familiar twang of a bowstring floated along the breeze as I leapt from the wagon and grabbed the first foe I could see.

The skirmish had ended as quickly as it had begun as I dropped the now drained, lifeless body of an orc, its blood dripping from my chin.

Looking around, the first thing I noticed were three other dead orcs scattered on the ground, one full of Loher's signature arrows, Byron and Balt standing near one each, blood dripping from their weapons and Sir Quinn, weapon drawn, within arm's reach of me; I must have stolen the one he was fighting.

I apologized to the knight and wiped my chin.

My secret was out now and I awaited a reaction.

The knight sheathed his sword, "I'm surprised I'm not more frightened than I actually am," he said as he feigned a laugh and slowly backed away.

"Frightened?" I asked, noticing the horrified looks on almost everyone's faces.

Loher slowly took a step toward me, her hands held out in front of her to show me that they were empty, "Take ease, my love," she said, stepping closer, "take ease and please don't..."

Before she could finish her statement, I noticed that there were rats surrounding my feet, my tongue ran across razor sharp teeth and my skin was starting to smoke; without thinking, I flew back into the shadows of the wagon's interior.

"...hurt me," she finished. "Where did he go?" She asked in surprise.

"Leave him be," Brother Fost calmly suggested, "there is smoke coming from inside the wagon; I believe he's in there."

"McLaaud, are you alright?" Loher called, "Please answer me!"

I checked myself for burns or any other damage and found that I was healing up quite quickly.

"I'm alright," I called back and then noticed that Loher was looking into the wagon.

There were tears in her eyes and a longing look on her face that showed that she genuinely cared for me.

"We're going to get you to Kennis and find out what we can to do bring you back to normal," she said with such conviction that I had no choice but to believe her.

"Narmal," Balt laughed.

"Rest easy now, son," Brother Fost said as he too poked his head into the back of the wagon, "it's a good thing that you just fed."

"Why's that?" I gurgled, my voice changing inhumanly.

"Several reasons," the priest answered, "for one, it will be a while until the sun goes down or until we get into the Tower. Two, I was beginning to become concerned with your diet, you have not been eating much lately, and finally, and I mean this with much respect, you're less likely to feed from one of us now."

"You know I would never..." I began to protest but the priest cut me off.

"So you knew what you were doing when you fed from that orc?" He asked.

I hesitated and lowered my head in shame.

I certainly did not intend to feed from that orc, nor did I even know what I was doing until after it was done.

Animal instinct had once again taken over until after I fed, making me realize that I was far more dangerous than I ever wanted to believe.

"What is the team's morale?" I asked, my voice turning back to normal.

"Shaken," the priest answered, "but I'm sure they'll be fine once you come out of here."

I gave him a puzzled look.

"Check your teeth," he said, pointing to his own mouth.

I ran my tongue across my teeth and felt that they had gone back to normal as well.

The sun didn't seem quite as bright and I could feel my heart beating again.

"Come now, McLaaud," Brother Fost offered his hand, "let us go show our friends that you're okay."

I smiled and tested the sun with my hand; no damage, so I crawled out.

I stood behind the wagon, shielding my eyes from the sun.

Loher was checking the bodies for what she liked to call 'goodies,' while Meeka and Kuchoff were gathering edible berries from the surrounding bushes.

Balt, Sir Quinn and Byron were collecting weapons and armor, bickering playfully about what should be taken or left behind.

"Did anyone find anything useful?" I called out to my friends.

The only answer I received was a dozen relieved smiles.

Back in the wagon, Sir Quinn and Byron up front, Loher and I looked through the 'goodies' that she had found.

As she emptied a pouch that she took from the lead orc, a handful of gold coins, eight or ten teeth and an old iron key fell into her lap.

We examined the key and found nothing of interest, but decided to keep it just in case it would come in handy in the Tower.

The other orcs only carried a few copper coins each, if that; they totaled seventeen in all.

Sir Quinn suddenly turned to look back into the wagon, "I have good news and bad news, which do you want first?"

"The good news," we all said in unison.

"The good news is that we can see the Tower," the knight explained.

"Wot's ta bad news?" Balt grumbled.

"The ground is too moist to continue in the wagon, so we're going to have to unhitch the team and lead them in on foot," Byron informed.

"How far is it to the Tower?" Kuchoff asked.

"Look for yourself," Sir Quinn said, pointing out in front.

The wagon slowed to a stop and we all poured out of the back.

The ground was mush beneath our feet.

Muck and filth oozed over the tops of our boots.

The wheels of the wagon were dripping with slop and were buried almost halfway to the axel.

Pushing the wagon proved to be next to impossible without using some sort of magic.

The Tower was about eight hundred meters* away through slop, mud, stagnant pest-infested water and quite possibly, quicksand.

(*just under a half mile or, just under one kilometer.)

"I have never tried to take a wagon through here before," Byron admitted, "but I do know the easiest way on foot. As I stated before, I have been here a few times hiding from bounty-hunters."

"Have you ever been **in** the Tower?" Loher asked.

Byron chuckled, "The main door of the Tower is locked, but I managed to find a few loose bricks that allow access to a small room, but the door in that room is locked as well, so it is best to say, no."

"I can tell you from personal experience, that there is no lock that Loher cannot open!" Meeka giggled.

Loher smiled, "It also helps that I may have found the key while searching those dead orcs," she said proudly, holding up the old iron key.

"Sometimes it pays to search the dead." Sir Quinn remarked.

"I have a feeling that this is going to be an interesting experience," Byron laughed.

"How so?" Balt inquired.

"This team is made up of some of the best fighters and magicians, not to mention an expert locksmith and a priest... and... let us not forget an immortal vampire!" Byron explained.

"A vampire that doesn't want to be a vampire, hence, the reason we are even going into the Tower." I moaned.

"Donna worry, Laddie," Balt spat as he clapped a hand on my back, "we'll git ye trew tis."

"I'm starting to overheat," I warned, "we should get going."

Trudging through the ankle-deep slop was, like trying to wade through knee-deep wet snow, difficult and slow going as the muck pulled at our boots.

Meeka, Loher, Kuchoff and Brother Fost mounted their horses in order to keep up with the rest of us.

We had asked Balt to do the same, but he refused, and kissed the blade of his Great Axe telling us that in case of an attack, he would be far more useful on the ground than on horseback.

After hearing that, Loher strung up her bow and Brother Fost readied his Blessed Crossbow.

Sir Quinn unsheathed his sword and inspected its blade with a smile, while Byron finally showed off the legendary Shino Sutoka Katana.

"So the legend **must** be true," Sir Quinn gasped when he saw the Shino Sutoka.

"What legend is that?" Byron asked with a raised eyebrow and a slight grin.

"Legend says that an elite Royal Soldier called Byron Le'Abboltt, once, with his own sword broken, fought a Fumetsu warrior to the death and won, claiming the legendary Shino Sutoka Katana as his own," Sir Quinn recited.

"My sword was hardly broken," Byron confessed. "You know, Fumetsu means 'immortal,' right?"

Kuchoff laughed, "Everyone knows that!"

"This Katana," Byron began as he raised his weapon for all to see, "only proves that they are in fact, **not** immortal."

The Tower now loomed ominously overhead as we struggled toward the front door.

Loher slid down from her mount and shouldered her bow.

"Let me check for traps and perhaps unlock that door," she advised, slowly making her way in front of the rest of us.

The elven maiden checked and found no traps, turned the key with a loud click...

Chapter Five

THE TOWER

A s if it was brand new, the large banded wooden door swung open easily, to let sunlight pour in and mingle with the flickering light of already lit torches.

The room was immaculate and smelled of incense.

"I'm sure it is obvious to all that we are definitely not alone in here," I muttered as we entered the Tower.

"Do you think I should close the door?" Brother Fost asked, a twinge of uncertainty in his voice.

"I think that would be wise," Loher stated, "Besides, I still have the key," she said with a smile as she pocketed the key for safekeeping and softly patted the spot where it rested with her hand.

"Be on yer guard," Balt rhetorically warned, grumbling under his breath.

"Where are the mounts?" Meeka asked.

"Safe outside," Kuchoff giggled, "I placed a Psi web around them, making them virtually invisible and very well protected."

"Psi web," Byron repeated quietly, shaking his head in amazement and wonder.

Our footsteps echoed as we made our way to the spiraling staircase in the center of the room.

"Before we go up," Loher cautioned, "I would like to check this room for any hidden doors or traps."

"Are you going to do that in every room?" Byron asked, captivated by the efficiency of the team.

"Probably," Sir Quinn answered with a smile, as the she-elf quickly looked around the room, "and you probably won't even realize that she's doing it."

"How often does she find something?" The veteran soldier asked.

"The last time we explored somewhere, it was a cave," the knight responded, "this is our first time exploring a built structure, so I'm just as interested to find out as you are."

"I guess it depends on how nefarious the builders wanted to be," Loher proclaimed as she made her way to the stairs. "Ready?" She asked as she checked each step on her way up.

We closely followed her lead, weapons drawn and ready to defend.

Loher was taking the lead, while Balt and Sir Quinn went next.

Kuchoff, Meeka and Brother Fost followed them while Byron and I took up the rear.

Once in a while, Loher would pause and study an odd brick or stone, but without a word, she would continue up the spiraling steps; I assumed that they were just odd bricks and stones as I never saw her use a tool to disarm anything like she did in the treasure chamber in the cave.

We reached the second floor of the Tower and Loher raised a hand to signal us to stop.

The room was filled with spider webs that hovered just above the floor.

New spider webs.

Thick strands.

"I got a bad feeling about this," Meeka whispered.

"H-how b-big w-would a sp-spider have t-to be to make w-webs **th-that** thick?" Brother Fost stammered.

Before anyone could answer, we all caught a slight bit of movement in the corner of the room to our close left.

The webs in the corner formed a sort of funnel type structure that stretched out and flowed into the room to create a messy sheet or blanket.

Within the funnel, the tips of the front two legs of a giant spider could just barely be seen.

"I recognize these webs," I cautiously stated in a whisper.

"How?" Byron asked.

"I'm a trained ranger," I answered.

The veteran soldier nodded his head in understanding.

"What kind of spider is it, McLaaud?" Loher asked, "Is it danger-ous?"

"The species of spider is known as a Tegenaria," I answered, "I will have to get a better look at her to see what subspecies she is to tell you if she's dangerous or not."

"A spider that large should be respected and assumed dangerous," Meeka suggested.

"Agreed," we all concurred.

"We have to get through this room to find Kennis," Sir Quinn announced, "besides, it's asleep and if we tiptoe over the webs, we won't get stuck in them."

The knight began to move throughout the webs, stepping over the lower and crawling under those that were too high to straddle.

Brother Fost, Balt and Kuchoff simply crawled on their hands and knees below the entire structure and made it through the room in record time.

Meeka, Loher, Byron and I began to follow Sir Quinn's lead by strategically stepping over the lower webs and ducking below the higher.

We were almost through when Meeka looked back and noticed that the spider had come out of her funnel and began to stalk us.

The wizard let out a stifled squeak of a cry that drew the rest of our attention, making Sir Quinn stumble and catch his arm on the webbing.

The spider, now recognized as a Tegenaria Duellica, was upon him with lightning speed.

Brown with muddy red and yellow in color, with eight long, skinny, hair covered legs and a slender, hairy abdomen, the spider was both beautiful and terrifying.

She pounced on Sir Quinn and engulfed him with her legs, pulling him under her.

The only thing we heard was a slight muffled scream and a loud bone-snapping crunch as she bit through the knight's armor and injected her poison.

The struggle was over well before it even began.

Stunned and shocked, we all just stood there for a moment, trying to make sense of what had just happened.

The spider began to wrap our dear deceased friend into a cocoon of webbing.

Suddenly a huge ball of fire erupted around the spider's head, accompanied by the angry and terrified screams of Meeka.

The wizard lobbed another fireball at the spider, then another.

"I killed him," Meeka sobbed, tears and snot running down her face, "I killed Sir Quinn."

She kept repeating the phrase.

(Another fireball...)

The spider ducked and tried to dodge the onslaught of the fiery evil, finally retreating back, away from the now cocooned corpse of the knight.

("I killed him.")

Balt began to hack away at the webs with his Great Axe as Loher began to fire arrow after arrow into the soft body of our foe.

(Yet another fireball...)

The dwarf's axe bounced harmlessly off of the steel-strong strands, but the she-elf's arrows were finding purchase and the spider screamed out in pain.

("I killed Sir Quinn.")

"We have to get out of here!" Byron called, "Kill that damned spider and let's go, before we attract even more attention!"

With tears streaming down her cheeks, Meeka summoned up every last ounce of her strength and cast an enormous energy bolt directly at the center of the spider.

The projectile soared across the expanse between herself and the spider and exploded on impact, sending shards of webbing, spider and stone adrift through the air.

"**Take cover!**" Balt yelled as we all ducked and covered away from the flying fragments.

("I killed Sir Quinn.")

"**I killed Sir Quinn!**" Meeka wailed out of control and then collapsed into a sobbing, convulsing, semi-conscious heap on the debris littered floor.

Byron quickly scooped Meeka into his arms and carried her out of the room while the rest of us followed behind, trying to keep from looking at the remains of the knight.

"We have to go back and get him!" Meeka cried.

"Tere's nuttin left o' him, Lass," Balt choked, "he got blowed up!"

"I killed Sir Quinn," Meeka quietly whimpered as we headed toward the next flight of stairs, Loher leading the way.

"We are in no condition for another encounter," Brother Fost warned, "I suggest we hole up somewhere and recuperate."

"I wholeheartedly agree," Byron added, in a soothing voice, trying his best to calm Meeka.

Loher and I took the lead and continued up the stairs as everyone else hung back on the stairs, prepared to descend to semi-safety, or to join us on the next level, assuming it is safe.

The third floor was well lit, again, by flickering torches, the scent of burning incense wafted about in the air.

The room was immaculate, as was the table in the corner of the room on the far side.

The table held a tome of sorts and I could tell that Loher was just itching to thumb through it.

(Such a curious creature.)

The she-elf quickly searched the room, the walls, the floor and what she could of the ceiling; she found nothing of interest, so she gave me the 'all clear' signal and I ushered the rest of our crew up the stairs.

"This seems like as good of a place as any to rest for a while," Brother Fost allowed as Byron gently set Meeka down near the tome.

Kuchoff and the priest quickly rushed to her side and began to make her as comfortable as they could, under the circumstances.

Balt began to work on smoothing out the now slightly dented blade of his trusted Great Axe, "Tat webbin' was as strong 'er stronger tan ta blade of me love 'ere," he said in surprise.

Loher, with her bow still in hand, began to flip through the pages of that strange tome that sat on the table in the corner, "I can't make heads or tails from this writing," she confessed.

"Perhaps Brother Fost can decipher it when he's done looking after Meeka," I pondered.

I checked through our supplies to see if we had any nourishment for Meeka, perhaps to make her feel better, as my own brand of hunger was beginning to act up as well.

I found some dried fruits and meat, as well as a few flasks of water; I offered it all to the priest and he accepted.

"She'll be just fine in a few hours," Brother Fost assured, "she's in shock right now, as I fear we might all be; we're just not as bad."

To be honest, I didn't feel as if I was in shock at all, and just by looking at Byron, I could plainly see that he was not in shock either.

After decades of wars for the old Tyrannical King, besides not knowing Sir Quinn the way the rest of us did.

Loher was in her own way, grieving on the inside, just as she tried to keep all of her emotions well within.

Balt had been trained from an early age, not to grieve the loss of a fellow warrior, but to celebrate the lives of those who had gloriously fallen in battle.

Kuchoff: the child, almost a young man now; it was difficult to know exactly how he was feeling at any given time of day as he always had that goofy toothy grin on his face, but the grin was now gone, perhaps from the worry for his new-found adoptive mother or for the loss of his friend; perhaps both.

Brother Fost: the priest, too busy at this time to even properly breathe, let alone grieve the loss of a companion that he had known for far longer than any of the rest of us; which brings us also to Meeka…

… Meeka: the wizard; she'll be feeling a guilt unlike any that she, or any of the rest of us, has ever felt or could ever even bear to feel.

A guilt that anyone would be reluctant to bestow on even the worst of one's enemies.

A guilt that is not rightfully hers to feel, as it truly was not her fault; blame it all on the dead, were he not to have rushed off ahead in such a hurry like he always did, he might still be alive today – but try convincing the wizard of that fact.

Perhaps in time she will understand.

(…The only thing we heard was a slight muffled scream and a loud bone-snapping crunch…)

As Meeka's sobbing subsided and the tower stood at a still, silence was the dominant sound around us.

The soft crackle from the torches would gently break the still momentarily, that is, if anyone paid close enough attention to even hear it.

We all had tried to eat something, if not because of hunger, then just to pass the time.

My own special degree of hunger had disappeared as I had found the occasional stray insect or rodent to satisfy the craving for blood.

Color had slowly returned to Meeka's face and her tears had all but dried up, she still had a wide-eyed shocked look on her face and she continued to stare off into space.

"Meeka," Brother Fost whispered…

No reply, not even a blink.

"Mom?" Kuchoff posed quietly, gently squeezing her hand to let her know he was still there...

... A small smile, then a blink.

Her eyes moved from the center to the left and then to the right; she blinked again and then looked around, her eyes finally settling on Kuchoff.

"I killed Sir Quinn," she whispered as a matter of a fact and the smile vanished.

"Ta spider kilt Sir Quinn, Lass," Balt quietly argued.

The wizard shook her head and looked down to her lap.

"It was an unfortunate accident, Meeka," Brother Fost murmured, "It's not your fault."

Tears welled up in her eyes, "I made him turn around and trip," she disclosed, "if I hadn't..."

"The spider would have gotten someone else," Kuchoff interrupted.

An angry look poured across Meeka's face and she began to rise, "Let's go find that old man and get out of here," she demanded through gritted teeth.

The rest of us shot bewildered looks at each other and rose to our feet as well.

"That tome," Loher remembered, "we can't forget that tome."

"Brother Fost," I coaxed, "would you take a look at this tome?"

"Perhaps either you or Meeka or Kuchoff can read what it says," Loher enticed.

The three learned companions gathered around the book and leafed slowly through its pages; questioning looks collected across all of their faces.

Unable to read the book, they all three agreed to take the book with us to see if Kennis himself could read the words within.

As the priest lifted the book from the table, there was a loud click from a room above us.

We all quickly shot each other worried looks as if to say, 'what now?'

Loher examined the table and found a pressure switch; she half giggled, "I guess I missed one."

Byron motioned his eyes in the direction of the stairs as if to say, 'no better time than the present,' and we all silently agreed and slowly started toward the stairs.

Loher, again, took the lead, checking for tricks and traps on the way and as usual, Balt went second, followed by Kuchoff, Brother Fost and Meeka with Byron close behind as sixth, while I took up the rear.

On the off chance that I was needed up front, with my vampiric speed, I could virtually be in two places at once.

With no tricks or traps on the stairs, we ventured slowly, cautiously onto the darkened fourth floor; my combination elven infrared and vampiric sight allowed me to see as if it was broad daylight.

The room was empty and void of any life.

Loher slowly made her way around and lit the torches, but only after she checked each and every one for traps; too many questionable things have already happened for us not to be extremely careful.

Now bathed in flickering firelight, she rechecked the room to no avail; satisfied, we continued toward the flight of stairs that led to the fifth floor.

As we reached the stairs, we could just barely make out an unidentifiable noise coming from the floor above; it sounded like... laughter, but we couldn't be sure.

We used our usual roster while climbing the stairs with Loher in the lead and myself bringing up the rear, and halfway up, we could discern that the noise we were hearing was in fact, laughter.

The laughter grew louder and more distinct as we gained altitude.

It was jovial laughter as opposed to maniacal ravings but our nervousness continued as we reached the top step.

I slipped up front to peer around the corner into the room, and what I experienced almost made my dying heart skip a nonexistent beat.

The stench of decomposing corpses and human excrement filled the room and wafted through the air; it was almost more than we could stomach.

The room was filled with cages, the doors on each ajar, most of which contained skeletons or rotting humanoid corpses; only one was empty, its door wide open and an old man was just outside of it, dancing a sort of jig and laughing.

Dressed in rags which used to be the clothes of a once much younger, healthier man, he was frail and looked unkempt; his beard, now grey, hung down to the middle of his chest.

His fingernails were long and were beginning to curl in filthy gnarls.

I raised my hand to signal the team to stay low and quiet as to not startle the old man; he had not noticed us yet.

We decided to stay put and observe him before making any further decisions.

His laughter continued and then slowly transformed into sobs, which in turn escalated into deep moans and convulsive fits of hysterics.

From this behavior, I assumed that he was the occupant of the only empty cage.

The old man's conduct continued for a matter of moments until it suddenly stopped and he whipped his head around to glare in our direction.

His eyes darted about, searching; his breathing became heavy, almost animalistic as he slowly crouched into a crawling position and cautiously eased his way toward us.

As he drew closer, we could hear that he was intently growling; saliva oozed through his gnashing teeth and dripped from his quivering lips.

"He's gone insane," Meeka stammered.

"Quiet, you!" Byron snapped in a hiss.

"He knows we're here already," Loher countered angrily.

"Perpare te d'fend yerselves," Balt growled and took a step forward, gripping his Great Axe.

I put my hand on the dwarf's shoulder and held him in his place; he looked up at me with surprise in his eyes and I soothingly shook my head 'No.'

Balt relaxed his ambition and allowed me to gently pull him back.

"Remember," I began, "we need him alive."

"Aye," Balt quietly agreed.

I stepped out unarmed and presented myself to the old man, my arms held open in an inoffensive posture, "Are you Kennis?" I asked in a confident tone.

The old man stopped and sniffed the air, his teeth stopped gnashing and his growl slowed to a stop.

"Kennis?" I repeated and held out a hand.

A look of wonder and familiarity of the name slowly trickled across the old man's face; he slowly straightened up into a standing posture and opened his mouth as if to speak –

-Before he could even utter one single word, a brazen, angry shriek came from a floor below us, "Someone has murdered my pet!!!"

"We gots comp'ney!" Balt sang out; it almost sounded joyous.

The old man withdrew back into his cage and the rest of us prepared for an attack.

⚬

Loher instantly engulfed Meeka and herself within her cloak and blended into the shadows of a darkened corner, while Kuchoff scurried into another and on his knees, began to chant some sort of Psionics.

Brother Fost readied his Blessed Crossbow and shielded himself behind Balt, who had anchored himself in a defensive stance; Great Axe also at the ready.

Byron took a running start at the nearest wall and gracefully scaled it with seemingly no effort, then perched himself in a large nook with his Shino Sutoka Katana ready to strike.

If I had not known that he was there, I probably would have never noticed him.

I positioned myself in front of Kennis' cage door and put my hands on my hips and just stood there defiantly as if I had absolutely no fear of what was about to take place.

"My tome," Kennis whispered behind me, "do you have my tome?"

"The halfling priest has got it," I whispered back.

"Give it to me," Kennis urged, "it can help us!"

"You can read it?" Brother Fost inquired as he slid the tome in our direction.

"Silly little man," Kennis cooed, "I wrote it."

I reached down and picked up the book and just as I did, a human woman bound into the room; her eyes glowing with anger and hate.

She was thin yet well-endowed and scantily clad under an open soft red robe; her dark brown hair flowed from her scalp like a brook and engulfed her shoulders.

In her left hand, she held a wand of some sort; I assumed at that time that it possessed magical properties as it was finely encrusted with tiny jewels and stones.

Brother Fost scrambled to hide again, behind our resident warrior and I handed the old man his book.

The sorceress took a step toward me.

"Tat be close enuff, Lassie," Balt growled and lowered his center of gravity.

From behind me, I could hear Kennis mumbling while flipping through the pages.

"You are trespassing in my home," the sorceress calmly conveyed.

"We are rescuing our friend," I countered in an equally calm tone.

"Your friend?" she questioned with a slight laugh.

"He is not our enemy, Madam," Brother Fost remarked from behind his live shield.

"Nor am I," the sorceress added.

"Yer 'pet' kilt our mate!" Balt growled through grit teeth.

"Hardly **my** doing," she defended with a smirk, "if you had not been trespassing, your friend might still be alive."

"If you were not holding Kennis against his will, we wouldn't have had to intrude," I countered.

The sorceress just stood there with a blank look on her face as if she had nothing to say to argue my point.

Kennis, behind me, could still be heard flipping through the pages of his book, giggling at times and mumbling what seemed to be random verses of odd poetry.

Balt was obviously losing his patience and began shuffling his position as if he was thinking about making a mad rush at the woman.

"I grow tired of this useless banter," the sorceress finally said angrily, yet with an anomalous smile drawn across her lips as she raised her jewel-encrusted wand.

A bright golden glow began to form around the tip of the wand as she began to draw circles with it in the air.

A slight breeze began to circulate within the room, kicking up the awful stench that I was just beginning to get used to, making it worse.

"Na our enemy," Balt sarcastically repeated as he stood his ground and prepared for the worst.

Suddenly, Kennis began to laugh, "It took a while, but I got it," he sang and recited a few lines of seemingly meaningless poetry.

Gradually, time began to slow until it completely stopped...

...The room began to spin...

CHAPTER SIX

OBSCURITY

Before I could even open my eyes, I felt as if the ground beneath me was rocking back and forth; not a completely unfamiliar sensation, yet one I do not particularly enjoy.

The air suddenly smelled and tasted sweeter and I could feel the wretched sun stinging the flesh on my face.

I felt as if, with whatever had happened, I had jumped out of the proverbial frying pan and into the almost literal fire.

I tried to open my eyes, but the pain was a bit more than I could take, so I shielded my eyes in the shadow of my hand and squinted to look around.

The first thing I saw was Byron, looking as confused as I felt and then laughter erupted around us; joyous laughter mixed with the sounds of lapping waves and creaking ropes.

I finally began to recognize the smell of salt in the air.

"I 'ave seen some strange tings, Mon, but to 'ave da lot o' yous jes appear on me ship is surplus!" A welcomed familiar voice laughed behind me.

"I have to get below deck," I urged as I turned around and began to rise to my feet.

"Not even a simple 'ello and a 'andshake first, Mon?" Captain Waxx laughed and helped me up, "Right dis way, Bruddah."

The captain led me to the stairs that led to the belly of The Scorpion.

I quickly shook his hand and thanked him as I scrambled into the more than welcomed darkness.

After a few moments of laying silently in the dark, I regained my composure and ventured back to the top of the stairs to gaze around at what I could see of the familiar ship.

"If you're looking for me, you're getting colder," I heard the old man cackle a few feet away from where I was just laying, "if I had realized that you were part vampire, I would have blinked you down here with me. I can help you with that, but, ahhh... you know this already. That is why you sought me out, my boy, am I right?"

"How did you know of this ship?" I asked, overly confused.

"This ship was the only common comfort spot in most of your minds," he answered within a chuckle, "with the exception of the acrobatic swordsman you recently added to your group."

"You read our minds?" I asked, astonished.

"Indeed, I did, my boy," Kennis laughed, "and let me thank you for rescuing me, my daughter will be quite pleased."

"Your daughter?"

"In due time, my boy, in due time. I must rest now, too much excitement."

I decided that I too should rest and wait until dark to explore and get some answers before the rest of my team retires for the night.

Not long after I found a comfortable spot to lie down and sleep, Loher had found me and curled up beside me and was soon in reverie as well.

So many unanswered questions...

My dreams at first were of the failed vampire hunter, Angelique DeStruere and Losian Sawol, the vampire that created the Hell I am 'living' through, but as dreams usually do, they drifted off to those of Sir Seth Quinn and the rest of my companions.

Soon to invade my head were those damn fairies riding the rabbits, but quickly switched to the battle with the Water Elemental on the very ship I was asleep on...

I opened my eyes and realized that Loher was no longer sleeping next to me.

The Scorpion was not rocking in its usual 'out to sea' manner and I could feel it gently bumping and rubbing against something solid.

I stood up and stretched a bit before going up the stairs into anticipated glorious moonlight.

The Scorpion was docked at a port, which seemed vaguely familiar.

I looked around and found my companions waiting for me in the ship's mess hall.

***

"Ever since this adventure started, we have gone through some fantastic and unbelievable situations," Brother Fost began as I walked into the room, "but earlier this afternoon as that sorceress was about to do Ohn only knows what to us, and then we suddenly found ourselves here, back on this ship, safe and all in one piece..."

"Let's go an get some eats," Balt cut the priest off with a light slap on the back and a grin, and then led the group onto the dock of Dewarg.

The priest just smiled and nodded his agreement, for his stomach was speaking louder than his voice.

There was an apparent chilliness in the night air as I observed Loher and Meeka pull their cloaks a bit tighter about their shoulders.

The night sky was brightly lit with uncountable stars, but no moon. No glorious moonlight.

This I found completely odd because the night before, the moon shown bright behind the wispy clouds that were now absent.

"This place looks so different at night," Kuchoff stated as he scampered past me and joined Meeka and Loher.

"I canna see a ting, Laddie," Balt added.

Candle flames danced in the shadows of the doorways and windows of the carved out dwarven homes, yet it was darker than I could ever remember, even with my vampiric vision as well as my infrared elven sight.

I could only imagine how poorly my companions could see.

The only thing we had to guide us up the steps to the town proper was the sound of the dwarves laughing and singing songs in the 'Ale House.'

As we got closer to the top of the steps, flickering torches were finally visible to guide us the rest of the way.

The music and singing grew louder as we approached the door to the 'Ale House' and I could almost see the tension from the stress of uncertainty melt away from my companions.

"First round's on me, Mates," Balt shouted over the noise as he opened the tavern door and led us in.

As we sat down in our usual spots at our usual table, I began to wonder why this particular table was always left open, as if on purpose, as if for us, but my attention was diverted back to reality when the barmaid, a human girl, arrived to take our orders.

She recognized Balt and graciously offered a discount for the night's refreshments as payment for a debt she owed him from a long time past.

Balt acted as if he was thinking long and hard to decide whether to accept the offer and then laughed in agreement, telling her that we would try to take it easy on the bill.

"I'll be back with your drinks momentarily," the barmaid promised with a low bow and then strode to the bar.

"What was that all about?" Meeka asked, "If you don't mind me asking."

"A few years back," Balt began, "I rescued 'er from certain death 'er worse when 'er village was attack'ed by a army 'o hobby-globlins."

"Hobby-globlins," Meeka giggled.

"She offers me ta same discount every time I comes inna here an she be workin'," Balt added, "an I always accept."

"So it's kind of like a game you two play?" Byron asked.

"I donna tink so, Mate," Balt answered after a moment's thought, "Methinks she be genuinely tankful tat I saved 'er an she dunno if she dun nuff ta pay me back even after I telled er tat we evenly squared."

"Do you need me to translate?" Brother Fost offered.

"No, Brother," Byron smiled, "I'm sure I understand."

I cleared my throat to gain the attention from all, "I think it's time for some information and a few answers," I announced, directing my gaze at Kennis.

The table fell silent and all eyes were on Kennis and me.

"I have a strong feeling I know what you're going to ask," Kennis relayed, "but go ahead, young man."

"I'm not sure where to start –" I began.

"You want to know who I am and where I'm from, you also want to know who my daughter is as well as how I can do what I have done, namely, getting us out of the tower and onto that ship, correct?" Kennis proclaimed.

"Y-yes," I agreed, astounded.

The whole group nodded their agreements as well.

"I know how you achieved the transportation from the tower to the ship," Meeka insisted.

"Of course you do, my dear Wizardess," Kennis winked, "of course you do, but the rest of our friends don't and I shall explain it all shortly, that is, unless you want to do it. "Be my guest," Meeka forced a smile with a glint of shame in her eyes.

Kennis lightly clicked his tongue at her as if to say, 'It's alright my dear, I forgive you.'

Meeka began to smile a true smile again and the glint of shame disappeared as if it had never been there at all.

As if on cue, the barmaid returned to our table with our drinks and a plate piled high with delicious looking cookies.

She set each drink down in front of the correct patron with impressive accuracy, announcing that the cookies were meant for the child, (Kuchoff,) but we were all welcome to enjoy them.

Kuchoff grinned at the barmaid and then licking his lips, he snatched up a cookie and began to eat it before the plate was even sitting on the table.

We all smiled and thanked her each dropping a few coins on the tray as a tip.

She beamed back at us brightly, bowed again and returned to her other guests.

"Most of your questions can easily be answered together with one answer," Kennis began as soon as we were alone, "that answer is: Shannon is my daughter."

Inquisitive looks appeared upon all of our faces.

"Let me explain with a little story, I can see now that my task is more difficult than I had thought it would be," Kennis chuckled and took a long pull from his drink.

"Shannon?" Byron asked with a raised eyebrow.

"Just listen," Loher scolded.

⸻◈⸻

"Byron, I know that you're new to this group of people, and you probably won't understand much of what you're about to hear, but please bear with me," Kennis began, "I'm sure that you'll understand after a moment or three."

"Go ahead," Byron agreed.

"Before you begin," Loher interrupted, "is it safe to assume that you're from the future plane, like Shannon and Jason?"

A look of both familiarity and confusion washed upon the old man's face, "Jason? I don't know of a Jason, but yes, Shannon is from a future plane, yet I'm not; I was born here in Beornan Heafod, in the town of Herostun."

"Herostun," Kuchoff giggled with a mouth full of cookie, "Quinn was from Herostun."

Meeka's existing smile lightly faded at the mention of the dead Knight's name, but soon returned to its former brightness as she remembered that children usually don't consider other's feelings when speaking of memories; they only convey the truth of the matter.

"Jason is a human male, around the same age as your daughter, that we met in the future plane along with her," Brother Fost explained.

"It's understandable," Kennis concurred, "it has been quite some... time, since I have been back to that plane."

"This is all quite interesting," Byron admitted, "I'm excited to learn the rest!"

"I'm surprised that you're not the least bit skeptical, my boy," Kennis declared.

"After some of the things I've experienced within my lifetime," Byron laughed, "it takes a lot to shock me."

"To be shocked is one thing," I offered, "to disbelieve is another."

"You all seem to be on the same level of belief," Byron explained, "who am I to call foul?"

"Fair nuff," Balt accepted for us all.

"Please continue, Kennis," I directed.

"As I said, I was born in Beornan Heafod around the time just before the Drow elves destroyed Dournan," Kennis attempted to begin again.

"But that was over three-hundred years ago!" Loher stammered, "There is no way—"

"Time travel, Loher," I reminded, "Please continue, Kennis, I'm sorry."

"No need to apologize, son, no need at all, I'm expecting more interruptions as the story goes on," Kennis laughed, "I'll skip to the part that matters."

Kennis took another long pull from his drink and then continued, "When I was about the age of twenty-five or so, I caught a sprite called Brendt, I'm sure you know of him."

We agreed silently.

"Brendt was so angry that he had been captured, he uncontrollably blinked us to the secret home of the fairies, causing even more trouble for himself, any questions yet?"

We all just sat there, intrigued by the old man's story.

"Well then," he continued, "as a punishment for the sprite and a quick way to fix the situation he had caused, namely me, we were both exiled to a future plane, but with the help of a coven of moon witches, we were returned back to this time."

"Where does Shannon fit into the story?" Kuchoff asked between bites of cookie.

Kennis laughed and almost spit up his drink, "You see, it took me such a long time to find the help I was constantly looking for, that I had met a nice woman, fell in love and started a family. It was years later, after she had prematurely died, that I found out that she was a moon witch and that our daughter, Shannon, had become a member of her coven."

"The Circle of Flowers," I added.

"Exactly," Kennis agreed.

"So the moon witches helped you return to our plane and back to your original life?" Meeka asked.

"As sure as I'm sitting here now," Kennis answered, "My mistake that put me in the tower was bringing one of the moon witches with me."

"The sorceress!" We all gasped together.

"The same," Kennis confirmed.

"Why did she trap you in that cell?" Brother Fost asked.

After a bit of hesitation, Kennis answered, "Because I had become more powerful than she, so she took my tome and tricked me into that cell, where I stayed ever since."

"How long?" Balt asked.

"Longer than I care to admit... Decades, or longer," Kennis frowned.

"So now that we rescued you," Loher excitedly began, "you can get McLaaud back to the coven and cure his..."

"Vampirism," Brother Fost completed, "just as they offered."

Kennis began to frown a bit deeper, "Did you happen to see the moon before we entered this tavern?"

"I noticed that there was no moon," I announced, "I thought that was a bit strange."

Chapter Seven

INLUNIUS

"Unfortunately," Kennis confessed, "I won't be able to help you without a visible moon."

"Let me guess," Byron cut in, "the sorceress stole the moon to deter you from helping us?"

"Precisely," Kennis validated.

"So how do we get it back?" Loher asked, close to panic.

"We kill the sorceress," Kuchoff answered with his signature toothy grin.

"Only after she returns the moon," Kennis corrected, "but we *must* confront her."

"What are we waitin' fer?" Balt growled and pounded his fist on the table, sending a few cookies into a low orbit.

"Take ease, my warrior friend," Kennis laughed, "this will be difficult, even for you."

"Bah!" Balt spat.

"We can do this." Meeka murmured, barely audible.

"Did you say something, Meeka?" I asked.

Meeka looked down at the table, "We can do this," she whispered.

"Speak up, Lass," Balt urged.

Meeka looked up with tears in her eyes, "We can do this," she hissed through clenched teeth, "for Seth."

"A fine vote of confidence, young lady, but—" Kennis started.

"Between my magic, your magic, Loher's arrows, and Kuchoff's Psi-skills," Meeka puffed, "we can do it!"

Balt growled again.

"I'm not forgetting you, Balt, or any of you," Meeka trumpeted, "I know that we can do this!"

"Fer Quinn!" Balt roared, temporarily gaining the attention of the other patrons.

"Quinn!" Kuchoff gleamed with a mouth full of cookie.

"Psi-skills?" Kennis retorted intrigued.

"You'll have to see it to understand," Meeka answered proudly.

The rest of us nodded in agreement.

Kuchoff seemed to glow with his own sense of inner pride.

Suddenly, Balt jumped up and like a streak of lightning, brought his Great Axe down on a dagger, in flight, aimed directly dead center at my back.

Byron drew his Shino Sutoka Katana and stood, ready to strike.

"It's a shame about your knight friend," a female voice projected from the shadows, "Sir Quinn, right? I kind of liked him."

"Show yerself, Assassin!" Balt growled.

"But you already know who I am," Angelique DeStruere laughed as she stepped into view, "the Monks were very helpful in tracking you down, so was the witch."

The vampire hunter took a full mug right from a patron's hand and proceeded to drink it, "I find it peculiar that I received help from both sides of good and evil, but who am I to refuse assistance? I must be well respected."

She slowly sauntered nearer to us, a defiant switch in her steps.

"Respect, huh?" Loher expressed, amused.

The vampire hunter glared at the she-elf, "You **will** respect me... or fear me."

"How about I just **kill** you," Loher barked as she dove at the huntress, dagger in hand.

Loher's dagger found purchase in the young woman's shoulder and the two combatants fell to the floor in a struggle to the death.

"All is fair in love and war!" Kuchoff shouted as he too, jumped into the fight, dagger in hand, but was quickly expelled from the scuffle by Loher.

⚬

"She's **mine!**" Loher snarled from somewhere within the dusty brawl.

"Donna git inna way, Lad," Balt chuckled, "wimmens kin be a wee bit feisty whilst fightin'."

A crowd of patrons, mostly dwarves, began to gather around the scuffle, shouts of encouragement were called out and even some coins were tossed into the 'ring' for the winner.

As we stood there watching the women wrestle around, with daggers, I noticed spattering of blood appearing within the slowing struggle.

The blood spots were growing larger...

Then, the fighting finally stopped.

When the dust settled and the crowd of patrons disbursed, both women were just lying there, covered in blood.

Then... Loher began to laugh.

She slowly sat up and spat out some blood and dust.

"Respect. Ha!" She said and then looked up at me with a confused look on her face.

The vampire hunter never moved.

I knelt down and took Loher's hand.

Helping her up, I embraced her in my arms and gently hugged her.

"I've been waiting a long time to do that." She whispered in my ear.

I wasn't entirely sure what she had meant by that.

I always assumed that she meant killing the huntress, but at times I wonder if she was referring to the embrace.

After a moment or two, she had finally had enough and smoothly shoved me slightly away, but never let go of my hand.

She pulled me toward the exit, calmly calling, "Would someone mind collecting those coins and paying for our bill please."

"Let me take a look at you," I said to Loher, pulling her closer, but she only shoved me away again, this time letting go of my hand.

She brushed herself off, "I'm fine, McLaaud, really," she argued and kept walking to the door.

"Brother Fost will want to…" I began, but I would have had to complete my statement to a closed door.

"I'll go talk to her," Meeka offered.

"Thanks, Meeka," I sighed.

"You may want to think about telling that to her," the wizard smiled as she too disappeared through the doorway.

"An' me," Balt grunted and lightly punched me on the arm.

"Thanks Balt," I croaked, "How did you know about the dagger?"

"A Mate o' mine signaled me at ta last second," the warrior admitted, "we dwarves gots our ways."

"We need to find the sorceress," Kennis reminded us in a whisper and lightly steered us to the exit from behind.

"Yeah!" Kuchoff whispered as well as he hurriedly led Byron to the door by the hand.

Byron shot me a helpless and almost embarrassed look as they passed us by.

Brother Fost was already at the door, digging out his book of healing, a worried look radiating upon his face.

Once outside I found my companions gathered near a grouping of torches, Brother Fost was inspecting and treating Loher's wounds.

"He says that she will be alright," Meeka informed, "a bit sore in the morning, but she should still be able to pull back her bow."

"Well, tat's guid news," Balt chuckled and nudged me with his shoulder.

"More good news is that you won't be stalked by that vampire hunter any longer," Byron added.

"We shall take a room at the inn," Kennis announced, "Master dwarf, will you lead the way?" he said and swept his arm in the air, gesturing to the path of flickering torchlight.

A crowd of patrons still lingered just outside of the tavern, chatting about the spectacle that had just occurred within.

Just as Balt was about to guide us on our way, two dwarven sentinels arrived and asked what happened.

While the rest of our companions told the story, Loher and I hung off away from them so my vampiric condition would not cause unnecessary prying.

They told the sentinels that Angelique was apparently an assassin, hired to kill Kennis, a trusted advisor to the King.

Byron was his son and bodyguard, Kuchoff was his grandson along for the journey, and the rest of us were their Royal escorts.

The Royal badges that the king had given us, before we explored the cave, and the story they told had succeeded in allowing us to move along on our way.

We immediately followed Balt to the inn and rented a few rooms.

Balt and Brother Fost shared one, Meeka and Kuchoff shared another, while Byron and Kennis took a third, leaving Loher and myself to share the fourth.

———— ❦ ————

Loher actually slept that night.

With the vampire hunter dead, she had nothing left to worry about.

I imagine it also helped her sleep knowing that I was 'awake' and watching over her, which brought forth a new problem...

...Daylight.

It was a good thing that we were in Dewarg, a town within a cave, because I would have burned up at first light.

Getting me from the town proper to the harbor almost became a problem.

For some reason that even Brother Fost and Kennis could not explain, covering me with a blanket to keep the sun off was just a temporary solution.

We finally stowed me below the decks of The Scorpion and set sail for the river to Loc Wepon, near Loher and my own home town of Larix, in the Seolfer Wudu.

"Capn' Waxx," Balt warned, "there be bridges on tat river tat we canna git under."

"Den we go as far as da bridges, Mon," Captain Waxx calmly explained, "an we take a dingy de rest of da wey."

"Yer ta dingy, Mate!" Balt growled, "Do I havta remind ya tat one of us be a VAMPIRE?"

Captain Waxx spun around to face the dwarf, an angry look upon his dark face, "Ya don't be needin' ta remind me, Mister dwarf," he spat, "I'm not likein' de idea of even havin' im on dis ship, but e's payin' me so I don't argue."

"Calm down, Gentlemen," Meeka cooed, placing a hand on a shoulder of each of the men.

Captain Waxx pulled away, "I'm not likein' de idea of womens and chillins aboard either, but ye saved 'er from dat water beast a few months ago, so I don't argue dat neder."

"What happened to you, Waxx?" Meeka asked, "You asked us to join with you if you remember."

"Bad tings 'appen when you all on board," Waxx confessed after a moment's pause.

"Well, I can't argue with that one, Meeka," Loher laughed as she stepped into view from behind a mast.

"Alweys sneakin' round," Captain Waxx muttered.

Loher pretended not to hear him.

"Come on you two," Loher coaxed, "let's go check on the others."

Meeka and Loher turned and began to walk away.

"Are you coming with us, Balt?" Meeka asked.

Balt grumbled something under his breath that made Captain Waxx have to stifle a laugh, and proceeded to walk away in the other direction.

Loher and Meeka ventured down the steps that led down below the decks, and as they did, they could hear some strange banging down below.

They quickened their pace in order to discover what and where it was coming from.

As they rounded a pile of loose boards and empty crates, they spied Kuchoff nailing boards together.

"What are you doing?" Meeka asked.

"It's a box!" Kuchoff smiled, excited.

"A box." Loher echoed.

"It looks more like a coffin," Meeka shivered.

"Good!" Kuchoff sang, "It's supposed to!"

"Why are you building a coffin?" Meeka asked.

"It's a box." Kuchoff sternly corrected.

"Okay, a box then," Meeka reluctantly agreed, "why are you build-ing it?"

Kuchoff stood up and brushed himself off, "I overheard what Balt and the captain were talking about, so I decided to come down here and build McLaaud this box, so the sun won't burn him in the..." then he giggled, "...dingy."

Meeka giggled too.

"That is very thoughtful, my young friend," I said as I sat up and stretched from my slumber, "and I thank you."

"You're welcome," Kuchoff smiled proudly, "did I wake you with my pounding?"

"No," I laughed, "I slept like the dead."

Kuchoff and Meeka giggled again, but Loher slightly frowned.

I shot her an apologetic look and then she half smiled too.

"You had better finish building that box, Kuchoff," I urged, "We will need to be using it soon."

"I'll make sure no sun can get through the cracks!" He announced.

Loher, Meeka and I smiled at the boy and silently excused ourselves to another portion of the ship.

Kuchoff's hammering echoed below the decks as we strolled away.

Moments later, the three of us were sitting on some crates, talking about what our plan of action should be against the sorceress, when Captain Waxx, Byron, Kennis and Balt showed up, "There you are," Kennis cackled.

"What ye be doin' Mates?" Balt asked.

"Discussing a sort of plan on how to confront the sorceress," I answered.

"Without us?" Byron teased.

"Where's Brother Fost?" I asked.

"Helpin' de boy make yor box, Mon," Waxx stated arching his right thumb backwards, over his shoulder.

"What plan did you come up with?" Byron asked, interested.

"Nothing, yet," Meeka confided.

"Let me take over," Kennis offered, "I know her better than she knows herself."

"Agreed."

"Well," Kennis began, "I'm sure we all know that in order to get close enough to the tower, we are going to have to bypass the bridge by going under it with a dingy."

Meeka and Balt smiled at each other as we all agreed.

"We are going to have to transport our undead friend," Kennis continued with a gesture toward me, "in Kuchoff's box, so the sunlight won't hurt him."

We all nodded our heads and Byron lightly clasped his hand on my shoulder as if to tell me it was all right.

"I have another idea!" Kuchoff called as he and Brother Fost carried the box to the group to show off the completed product.

"Pray tell, young man," Kennis urged.

"When we get to dry land, someone can go ahead of everyone with me to fetch our horses," the boy proposed, "they should still be there in my Psi web."

"Psi web?" Kennis asked.

Byron just smiled and shook his head, as he did the first time he heard those words, "I'll go with you, Kid," he offered.

"I'll go too," Meeka insisted.

"Psi web?" Kennis repeated in confusion.

"It's difficult to explain, Kennis," I assured, "you just have to experience his abilities in order to even slightly begin to comprehend the whole 'Psi' thing."

Kennis shook it off and continued, "As you three go off and retrieve the horses, the rest of us will do our best to carry the box to the tower and you will meet us as soon as you can."

"What about when we meet up with you?" Meeka asked, "How will we transport the box? On horseback?"

"That depends on how close we are," I answered, "and what the terrain looks like."

"What are you thinking," Byron cut in, "building some sort of cart to pull you behind a horse?"

"It's a thought," I responded.

"Meeka," Loher entered, "couldn't you just 'blink' him to the tower?"

"NO!" Kennis pounced, "The sorceress would detect the magical energy and then there goes our element of surprise."

"Good point," Meeka agreed.

"Why don't I just cover with a blanket and run as fast as I can," I offered, "I **am** a vampire after all."

"What about when you get to the tower?" Brother Fost asked.

We all just looked at each other with confusion and shame washing across our faces until Loher shattered the silence, "I still have the key!" She reached into her pouch and produced the old iron key.

"Let me see that!" Kennis gasped and held out his hand.

Loher looked at me for guidance and I nodded.

She reached over and dropped the key into the old man's hand.

Kennis looked the key over and began to smile, "Do you know what you have here, my dear?" He asked as he gave the key back to her.

Loher shrugged her shoulders, "The key to the tower's front door?"

"The tower's **master** key!" The old man smiled, "That key will unlock every door within the structure! The secrets that can, and will be revealed with that key are far beyond anything that any of you can ever imagine!"

"Well," I began, "as far as I'm concerned, the key is all yours after we get the moon back and I can return to my former living self again."

The old man was drooling over the thoughts within his head.

"So what happens after we all meet in the tower?" Byron asked, returning Kennis back to reality.

"We go confront the sorceress," Kuchoff sang.

"Easier said than done, my boy," Kennis laughed and mussed the Psionisist's hair, "leave that to me, I'll fill you in when we get there."

We reluctantly left it to him, he did in fact, know the sorceress and her ways.

The journey inside of Kuchoff's well-built box started off with a terrible thud as the dingy carrying the box (with me in it) was dropped the last few meters into the river after being lowered over the side of the ship.

Afterwards, the only thing I experienced was the nice, soothing rocking back-and-forth motion of the waves.

I must have fallen asleep for most of the journey, as I was awoken by the sound of Loher's voice...

"McLaaud," Loher called, "I can hear the horses, they're close, are you ready to come out of your box?"

Loher had given me the tower key before I crawled into Kuchoff's box, six hours ago.

I was already wrapped in a thick woolen blanket that we had 'borrowed' from the inn in Dewarg; Balt intended to return it.

"It's kind of cozy in here," I teased.

Loher kicked the side of the box... hard.

"I'm ready, I'm ready!" I laughed.

My laughter was short lived as she pried the lid from the box, and poison sunshine washed over me like the burning flames of the Underworld.

I stood bolt upright and began running as fast as I could; in the exact direction, Loher had pointed me.

Less than a second later, I could smell and hear the horses as we passed each other by.

The horses never even knew that I had passed.

If I counted correctly, twenty-four seconds later, I was standing comfortably in the shaded entrance of the tower.

And I waited...

And waited...

Waited...

Wait...

Almost two hours later, (I would have burned up for sure) my companions walked up to the door on foot.

"Where are the mounts?" I asked.

"Psi web," Kennis and Byron echoed each other, Byron, hooking a thumb back over his shoulder.

Meeka began to giggle, followed by a very proud looking Kuchoff.

Loher and Brother Fost both looked relieved to see me in one piece.

Balt just nodded and plopped down on a dead stump near the door, "Sorry it took so long, Mate," the dwarf breathed, "I telled 'em na te wait fer meh."

"We are all together now and that is all that matters," I calmly assured.

My companions gave each other a little bit of time to calm down and recover from the two-hour journey through the swamps.

"It's going to get dark soon," Byron announced.

I turned to look at Kennis, "What is the plan from here on?"

"The sorceress will most likely be in the highest portion of the tower soon after sunset," he said, thoughtfully, "but with the moon in the state that it's in, I'm unsure of what she will be doing."

"This is probably going to be a dumb question, but what does the moon have to do with what she does at any certain time?" Loher asked.

"She is a moon witch," Kennis explained, "therefore, almost all of her rites and rituals are based on the moon."

"So moon witches be evil," Balt guessed.

"Most contrary, Master Dwarf," Kennis corrected, "Most witches from all walks of life are usually neutral in nature."

"So she just went power mad," Meeka deduced.

"Correct." Kennis concurred.

From above, we could see that the sunlight was getting dimmer and nighttime descended about the tower.

"It's almost dark, McLaaud," Byron whispered and placed his hand on my shoulder, "are you ready?"

"Ready for what?" I half laughed, "We still have no plan."

"I may have one," Kuchoff declared in an undertone.

There was a thoughtful look upon the young boy's face; his usual toothy grin had been replaced by a more serious, almost astute demeanor.

Meeka's smile suddenly disappeared, "Psi time?"

Kuchoff's eyes lit up as he looked at us and nodded his head.

Byron and Kennis shifted in their stances and began to look a bit nervous.

"Kennis," Kuchoff inquired, "I need you to tell me everything that you know about this woman. Every detail."

The old man chuckled, "Well that could take some time, my boy."

"Well then, you'd better get started," I urged quietly, yet sternly.

The oldest member and the youngest member of our group moved into a secure corner of the room and began their meeting as the rest of us stood guard, weapons and wits at the ready.

What seemed like hours passed as the Psionisist and the old man discussed the sorceress; looks of confusion and understanding waltzed back and forth from old face to young face and at times their faces even seemed to merge into one.

Meeka had disappeared into the tower for a moment, but returned looking a bit shaken, but all the while, smiling.

"Where have you been?" Loher asked the wizard, pulling her aside.

The wizard produced Sir Quinn's sword and Royal badge, "I'm going to give them to Kuchoff." She announced.

"I'm sure he would appreciate that." Loher commented.

We knew the meeting was over when the young boy and the old man turned to me and asked if I was ready.

"I am," I answered, "but before we go, Meeka has something for you, Kuchoff."

Meeka presented the boy with her gifts of the Royal badge and the castle forged blade.

He took them and proudly placed the badge on his chest.

The sword was almost a bit too long for him to strap to his belt, but somehow he made it work.

"Now we're ready." I stated.

CHAPTER EIGHT

THE TOWER - REVISITED

After a brief meeting between the eight of us, we had come up with a plan that some of my companions were not sure would work as well as expected.

Darkness had finally fallen around the Tower and we decided that with no fear of the harmful sunlight to destroy me, this was as good of a time as any to carry out the plan.

Loher and Meeka hid beneath Loher's cloak and camouflaged into the rock wall; they blended in so well that even those of us who knew where they were, still could not see them.

Meeka began to summon her magical pet mouse to serve as a spy.

With a slight puff of pink mist, the mouse appeared near the wall and quickly scurried off to find the sorceress.

Balt quietly laughed and went to stand guard at the entrance, Great Axe in hand and a stern look upon his leathery brow.

Byron wished us all luck, drew his Shino Sutoka Katana and virtually disappeared into one of the various nooks of one of the walls.

"I'm willing to bet that he was trained by some sort of ninja or something of that nature," I commented.

"You would win that bet," Byron's disembodied voice quietly answered.

At this same time, Brother Fost had begun setting up a makeshift triage, just in case someone was injured, due to a lack of proper planning.

Kennis dug out his all too precious tome, and began to research a way to steal back the moon from the sorceress' spell, a way to reverse it if possible, while Kuchoff and I stood and waited for the sorceress to be found.

"Between Meeka's mouse and our resident contortionist, one of them should find her fairly soon," Brother Fost mentioned as if reading my mind.

According to plan, Meekas's mouse finally located the sorceress and returned instantly with the news.

With seemingly one single word, Kuchoff, Kennis, Byron and I were 'blinked' into the room full of cages; Byron, back to his hiding spot that he had occupied the first time we encountered the sorceress, and the three of the rest of us, into a cage.

Kuchoff used his Psi Skills to make himself appear to be a baby ogre, because according to Kennis, the sorceress had always wanted to capture a baby ogre to train to be her bodyguard and now she will think that she finally has that chance.

Kuchoff's Psi Skills, at the same time, were to mask Kennis and myself, showing only the illusion of the ogre child.

We never sorted out a reason why the ogre would be in the cage and we hoped the sorceress' excitement would be enough to distract her from thinking about it.

Meeka's 'blink' spell should be enough to alert the sorceress of magic usage within the tower walls and she would have no choice but to investigate.

<hr>

The plan began to work perfectly.

Before we knew it, the sorceress' head peeked around the corner that opened to the stairs leading to the top of the tower.

Upon spying the ogre child in the cage, the sorceress' eyes went as wide as two full moons, but she still cautiously looked about the room to see if they were alone.

Satisfied that they were indeed alone, she made one last effort to detect any magic usage within the room.

Kuchoff's Psi Skills however, were not magically based and therefore undetected by her spell.

Completely satisfied that she was safe, the sorceress ventured into the room and strolled up to the cage door, "Well, hello there, beautiful!" The sorceress cooed at Kuchoff.

Kuchoff stayed silent and just stared at the woman with feigned fear in his ogre- like eyes.

"Where did **you** come from?" She rhetorically asked.

Again, Kuchoff stayed silent, only whimpered as the ogre.

From where I was positioned, I could see Byron, silently creeping up behind her.

The sorceress took the bait!

As she took a step into the cage, Kuchoff, posing as the ogre, began to cry to distract her further as Byron closed and locked the cell door behind her.

Not needing the Psionics any longer, Kuchoff released control and the three of us appeared before her.

I grabbed the woman with my vampiric strength while Kuchoff quickly stripped her of anything that may be of magical value, like rings, charms, her wand and anything else in her (nonexistent) pockets.

All of the magical items were then tossed to Meeka, who conveniently happened to rush into the room, along with Balt and Loher.

I picked her up, gripping her arms tight enough to restrict the blood flow and leave bruises, "What have you done with the moon?" I growled at her, shaking her a bit.

She winced in pain but stayed silent; the frozen look of fear engulfed her face.

I bared my fangs at her and hissed.

"Take ease, my boy, take ease and put her down," Kennis laughed, "there are more ways than that to get what we came for."

The sorceress rubbed her now raw, bruised arms and looked around the room after I roughly tossed her back to the floor.

My whole entire group suddenly surrounded the cage, angry looks across each and every face.

"I am only going to ask you once to restore the moon to its former glory," Kennis calmly announced, "do it now and we will let you live. If I have to ask again, I will not just simply ask, I will torture you until you comply and then my vampiric friend here, will change you like he is and you will exist in misery, within this cage, hobbled and broken for the rest of eternity."

"It's your choice," I said, licking my fangs, secretly hoping that the old man wasn't serious, "but I hope you fight us," I stuck my face less than an inch from hers and breathed, "I because, **I'm hungry!**"

The sorceress dropped to her knees and began to quiver and cry.

"Watch yourselves," Byron warned, "it might be a trick!" he placed the edge of his katana's blade a few inches from her neck.

Kennis looked at Byron and shook his head, "We need her alive," he counseled, "for now."

Byron withdrew his blade.

The now powerless sorceress continued to cry, but never made any sudden movements.

"I grow impatient, My Dear," Kennis warned and attempted to help the woman to her feet through the bars of the cage, but she went limp legged and collapsed to the floor, landing on her rump with a jarring finality.

"Just kill me," she cried, "I'll never help you."

"This is not like you to just give up," Kennis laughed, "why is stopping us so important to you?

The sorceress looked at Kennis with flaming hatred in her eyes, "You brought me here against my will, you bastard!"

"Against your will," Kennis full out laughed, "it was **your** idea to come to this realm in the first place!"

"I just wanted to be with you!" She cried.

"I am but a shell of the man I used to be," Kennis countered, "return the moon to the way it once was and you may return to your home once again."

The woman's eyes lit up at the sound of this offer.

"But," Kennis continued, stroking the bars of the cage with his fingers, "on second thought, I don't think I could ever forgive you for locking me in this cage like you did."

The light in the sorceress' eyes suddenly smoldered to ash, "There is a special place in the underworld for you." She sobbed and dropped her head down again.

Kennis growled and stomped his foot, "Perhaps you will join me there," he sneered, then, after a long pause, he looked up, "Byron," Kennis ordered, "open the cell door."

The Shinto Master complied and then backed away from the open cage door.

"Okay, McLaaud," Kennis urged, "your part will come soon, but for now, I need you to pull her out of here."

Without hesitation, I grabbed the sorceress up, by the hair and drug her, kicking and screaming out of the cage.

With a slight gleam in his eyes, Kennis swiftly grabbed the sorceress by the neck and forced her to the window.

We were several levels up, if she were to go through that window, it would mean certain death.

Meeka began to whimper, seemingly for the sorceress.

Kuchoff scampered to her, took her hand and attempted an infectious smile.

Hanging the sorceress half way out of the window, Kennis politely asked, "Now, my dear, if you would be so kind as to return the moon?"

The sorceress wiggled herself around enough to spit in his face.

Her agility took the old man by surprise and he (accidentally?) let loose his grip.

The sorceress was silent as she slipped over the window ledge and plummeted to the ground with a soggy impact.

"Heared tat one hit da ground, eh Priest?" Balt chuckled.

The halfling priest failed to stop the smile that lightly formed across his lips.

"I don't think she's dead." Byron reported from the window.

"She soon will be," Kennis replied as he scanned through his old magic tome, "her body is broken and it won't be too long until an alligator or some other creature finds her and makes a fine meal of her flesh." Kennis assured, "but by all means, if you feel it important enough, you could run down there and put her out of her misery."

Byron just shook his head in disgust and walked away from the window.

I began to wonder what exactly, I had gotten my friends into.

With the sorceress dead or dying and the moon still nowhere in sight, would this old man be able to fulfill what legends say he can?

We waited in silence, other than the weak moans of the woman on the ground far below, for what seemed like hours as the old man looked through his book, Kennis suddenly called with a smile, "I have found what we are looking for! "Looks like we don't need you after all, my dear!" He shouted out the window as he slammed the book shut and returned to the group.

We all just stood there looking at him blindly.

"Follow me up to the top."

<hr>

The top level of the tower was filled with piles of coins, gems and trinkets of all sorts, from every corner of the realm.

Things of beauty and items of rarity were leaned up against the walls.

Weapons and armor of all shapes and sizes were stacked in heaps along with chests of every type of currency imaginable.

"Do help yourselves, my friends," Kennis urged, "take it as payment for letting me out of that infernal cage."

My party began to look around, first at each other, then at the wondrous things to behold.

Byron had found an old dagger that looked similar to one he had as a younger man, before he joined the Royal Army.

He held it up and inspected it with memories of years past within his head.

"Meeka, My Dear," Kennis called soothingly, "I do hope you still have the sorceress' wand."

Meeka forced a smile and produced the wand, "I have these rings as well," she said, holding out the rings.

"Keep them," Kennis said as he gently closed her fist around the rings, "as a token of my appreciation for all of your help."

Meeka let a genuine smile escape her lips as she turned away and sat back where she was.

She inspected the rings one by one and noticed that each one had a unique power, all of their own.

She vowed to research them and discover what each one did; perhaps she could use them herself.

If not, they would probably fetch a nice price in a shoppe somewhere.

Loher found a long bow made of a very light, but unidentifiable wood.

She pulled the bowstring back with greater ease than she could with her own.

Notching an arrow to the string, she pulled back once again and let the arrow fly.

The arrow found purchase in the solid rock wall without cracking the stone around it.

She decided that she preferred this bow over her own and shouldered it, keeping her old bow, just in case she still needed it.

I witnessed these events and decided to take a look for myself.

I searched through the contents of the room, but nothing seemed of any interest to me until my hand brushed up against a cloak made from the softest linen mix I had ever felt.

I had no idea what the linen was mixed with to make it so soft.

The cloak itself looked as if it were spun out of actual shadows.

I put it on and Brother Fost gasped.

"What is it, Brother?" I asked, but the priest's eyes just darted about, searching in my direction.

"You, you disappeared!" He said a half smile on his halfling face.

I removed the hood from over my head and the priest's eyes seemed to snap focused back on me.

"That's amazing!" Brother Fost cried in glee.

I decided that perhaps this cloak just might come in handy someday.

"What did you find for yourself, Brother Fost?" I asked.

"We priests have no use for that sort of magic," he simply stated with a grin and a slight chuckle.

Balt had found an impressive sharpening stone that kept his Axe as sharp as it was when it was newly forged.

Kuchoff managed to find a suit of light weight scale armor that fit him quite well with room to grow.

"Now that you all have had time to pick out your rewards for such a fine job done," Kennis laughed, "we can get on with the task of restoring the moon for all to enjoy once again!"

"Then perhaps, restoring my maritus to his former living self," Loher muttered.

"Indeed," Brother Fost quietly agreed, "that shall be my reward."

Kennis smiled at Loher, blinked a few times and then turned to his tome.

He raised the former sorceress' wand in the air and began to recite what sounded again, like odd poetry.

After several verses, the words began to take shape in my head and I could almost understand the meaning behind them and at that exact same time, a spot in the night sky began to glow and get brighter.

The moon was returning!

Meeka turned and looked at the rest of us, a pleased grin etched on her lips, "See now," she said, "I knew that we could do it!"

Even from the top of that very tall tower, we could begin to hear the sounds of life far below begin to take charge of the night.

Swamp creatures moved through the slime while the woodland critters scurried around and hunted for their late dinners.

Eventually, we heard the distant screams as a swamp creature found the dying sorceress.

She was, no more.

But, before any of this happened, it had never occurred to me how important the moon is to the world and how precious **innocent** life actually is.

Kennis looked back out into the moonlit night and seemed to lose himself in it.

He stood there, unblinking, thinking.

It suddenly looked as if he was trying to make the most impossible decision of his life and the choices that he had carried life as well as death upon them.

Finally, a look of pure clarity washed over him and he began to breathe.

His eyes narrowed and then blinked a few times and then he slowly turned his head and looked directly at me.

"Are you ready to become human again?" He asked.

"Kennis," I cautiously began, "I was only half human."

"Well," the old man laughed loudly with a huge smile upon his face and put his hands on my shoulders, "you know what I mean, my boy, you *do* want to be **alive** again, don't you?"

"Yes," I calmly answered, "yes I do."

"Well, then, let's go do just that!" He cackled as he jovially guided me down the stairs toward the front door.

⸺◆⸺

We knew instantly when we got to the floor where Sir Quinn had died because there was rubble and thick webbing all over the room.

A large, gaping, charred hole was still smoldering and smoking near the door we had to go through.

"Close your eyes, Meeka," Byron warned, "you're probably not going to enjoy this."

Meeka stopped, and her face suddenly contorted into a grizzly frown.

The wizard slowly turned around and threw her hands into the air...

POP!

We found ourselves standing near the river by The Scorpion's dingy, pink mist evaporating into the night breeze.

The moon was shining brightly and I could see through the night just as well as I used to be able to see in the day.

"Wizard," Balt spat, "why dint ye tink o' tat earlier?" He then began laughing with a defiant tone.

"Do dwarves know **anything** about magic?" Meeka rhetorically asked as she quickened her pace toward the ship.

"I'm bettin' I knows mar'n any ot'er dwarf be knowin'." Balt called after her.

Meeka just smiled without turning around and continued her trek to the ship.

I looked up the river and felt relieved when I saw the lights from the lamps aboard The Scorpion, which was docked just on the other side of the bridge.

"Right where we left her," I thought out loud.

Loher turned and looked in the same direction and smiled as well.

She gently took my hand and began to guide me to the dingy.

"At least I'm not in a box this time," I quietly snickered and followed her.

"At least you're not in a box this time," Kuchoff called to me, laughing, "right, McLaaud?"

"Right, Kid," I called back, "get in the boat."

Kuchoff smiled and scampered to the dingy and surprisingly enough, the new scale armor he was wearing made no sound.

When we finally reached The Scorpion, Captain Waxx was there to welcome us aboard, "Was it juss my imagination, Mon, or did I 'ear some scary screamin' comin' from de swamp?"

"You could hear that?" Kennis laughed, slightly surprised.

The captain nodded his head and helped the old man board, "Sound carries in de swamp, Mon."

"Hi Cap!" Kuchoff piped as he scrambled up the rope ladder and hopped up onto the deck.

The captain's eyes met Meeka's as she was the next up the ladder, "Ma'am," he greeted and took her hand, "my 'pologies for earlier," he helped her to the deck, "you be welcomed aboard."

"Thank you," she chirped.

When we were all finally aboard, Captain Waxx began to shout out orders and the crew, like a well-oiled machine, took The Scorpion back out to open sea.

"Where we be headin' to dis time, Mon?" Captain Waxx asked as he strolled up beside me; I was looking out to sea, remembering when I was alive and on the way to the yet unexplored cave for the first time.

Things were so different back then, I had never been so far away from Larix before and moreover, I didn't know my companions as well as I did now.

Could I trust them?

Yes, with my life. (And after.)

Would they trust me?

Yes, more than I ever thought possible. (Especially as a vampire.)

Will we make it?

...I miss my horse.

"I'm not sure," I answered the captain, "you should go talk to the old man."

Captain Waxx's dark face went ash grey, his eyes began to bulge from his skull and I could tell that his mouth suddenly went dry.

"What is it Mario?" I asked, concerned.

"De ol' man," The captain groaned, "gives me de creeps."

"I'll go with you," I offered.

The captain forced a smile and silently agreed with a slight nod of his braided head.

I took a quick look back out to sea and then led the way down below to where the old man liked to sit and ponder things... I hoped he was there.

As we walked to the steps that led down below decks, I marveled at the efficiency of The Scorpion's crew; they knew exactly what needed to be done, when to do it and how to do it.

The men sang a chant like tune in deep but rhythmic voices that reminded me a bit of the monastery that we found Byron in.

I refuse to believe that the monks had told Angelique where we had gone, mainly because we never told them where we were going and they never asked.

She lied to us.

We had simply been escorted out of the building and **wordlessly** sent away, why would things be any different with her?

It doesn't take a scholar to figure out that a tower such as the one near the monastery would be a perfect place for a hunted vampire to hide.

There is, however, one thing that is confusing me on this matter; how did she know about the monastery in the first place?

Thoughts for another time.

As Captain Waxx and I descended the steps into the belly of the ship, I found Kennis right away, sitting in his usual spot, sharing a pipe of tobacco with the First Mate.

"The captain would like to know where we are heading now," I relayed to the old man.

Kennis smiled, rose to his feet and brushed himself off, "We'll have to take the long way 'round, due to the bridges," Kennis puffed, "but we should head to Avilyn Harbor. I'll tell you the rest when we get that far."

Delighted to have received new bearings, the captain hurried back up the steps as fast as he could go and began to shout out orders to the crew.

Why the secrecy though?

What was Kennis hiding, or was he just as lost as the rest of us?

CHAPTER NINE

NON LINEAR

Getting back to what I was saying about how important the moon is to life; apparently it is quite important to the weather as well, because as calm as the open sea was on our way to Dewarg and then to the Tower, it was the exact opposite on our way to Avilyn Harbor and we were sailing the exact same route, only a few hours later.

Waves almost as tall as the railings were washing aboard; soaking the decks, but the expert crew of The Scorpion overcame the turbulence and navigated through it as if it were mere child's play.

My companions were all sleeping or resting up for the next chapter of our adventure, or at least they were trying to as the ship rocked back and forth on the ever growing waves.

I stood there, gazing at the bright stars that guided us over the sea, finding new respect for the crew of The Scorpion and their knowledge of sailing and star navigation.

I couldn't imagine being on board a ship for more than a few days at a time, but these men lived most of their lives on this floating scorpion shaped statue.

In my opinion, it takes a lot of courage to face the open sea for months on end, perhaps even years.

These men seemed to enjoy it though; they have dedicated their lives to the captain and this ship.

It only seemed like a short moment in time as I stood there, peering out into the darkness of the sea, but my special breed of hunger was telling me otherwise.

Hungrily, I scanned the horizon to see if I could see land, but only saw the faint shimmer of the sun about to peek over the waves.

I had to feed soon and then get below decks.

This was the worst place for a vampire to be; aboard a ship with mortal people who trust him and no stock to feed from.

We should have prepared for this.

I stood there thinking about what my options might be and I came up with a possible solution.

I could either feed from the rats that were constantly scurrying about my feet or I could seek out the mess hall.

The mess hall should have something alive for me to feed from, so I silently made my way past the ever present crew and slipped inside.

"I was wondering when you were going to show up," the cook said as he saw me come in.

He was a large, burley human man with a slight dwarven accent but no discernible dwarven attributes besides the curly reddish hair and ruddy cheeks.

He was also much too tall.

He had fear in his eyes, but not the terrified kind; it was calm, almost as if he was ready for me to attack.

There was a large wooden stake within arm's reach of him and a large wooden mallet as well.

I smiled when he saw that I had noticed his defenses and simply tapped on the armor chest plate under my tunic.

The fear in his eyes went wild and he began to slowly inch his way into the corner.

I took a big step back, "I'm not here to harm you," I said calmly and raised both of my hands in a non-aggressive manner.

This seemed to calm him down to the point of fear that he had when I arrived.

"It's blood you need then," he pronounced in a shaky voice.

I nodded my head.

"I think I have just the thing for you," he smiled falsely and turned to a door at the side of the room.

He opened the door and retrieved a large sack that contained something alive; I could see the shape moving inside.

The cook set the sack on the table and excused himself, "I don't want to be in here to witness this."

He scrambled past me and out the door as my eyes fixed upon the moving sack on the table.

I could hear it breathing.

A strong heartbeat.

What is it?

I slowly made my way to the table and grasped the drawstrings on the sack.

The creature inside began to move a bit more.

I loosened the knot and opened the sack to reveal a feral boar, its snout tied shut and legs bound with a leather cord.

My hunger grew more intense.

I took a quick look back at the door to make sure no one was watching.

I was alone.

With lightning speed, I sank my fangs into the boar and drained every last drop of blood from its squirming body.

I felt stronger, satisfied.

Before I left the mess hall, I neatly cleaned up any blood that I may have spilled and loosely tied up the sack.

I opened the door and walked out, "Looks like the crew is having bacon for breakfast," I chuckled at the cook as I walked by.

The look of horror and disgust on the cook's face was well worth the foul taste of swine on my lips.

The darkness below decks was beckoning me, so I made my way to the steps and escaped the rising sun.

When I arrived at the bottom of the steps, Kuchoff and Kennis were playing some sort of game on the floor while Meeka sat on a crate and watched.

They seemed so comfortable with each other.

They didn't even notice me as I silently slipped past them and retired into Kuchoff's hand-made box that I decided to 'sleep' in.

As I drifted off into peaceful slumber, I could hear them laughing and having a good time.

It warmed my un-beating heart to hear the laughter of a child.

My dreams were those of Stahvee and my home in the Seolfer Wudu.

I wondered if I would ever see that place again.

⊙

I was awakened by Loher as she stood a few feet away and tossed rocks at my den.

This made me laugh, but one can never be too safe when dealing with a waking vampire.

I was glad that this wouldn't be the case for much longer... hopefully.

The sun was only moments away from dipping below the horizon and I preferred to be awake for as long as possible; Loher knew this and woke me every evening.

She too would rest as much as possible in the daytime so she could be alert in the night with me.

Avilyn Harbor was only a few hours away now and we were all eager to disembark into the next leg of our mission to restore my soul.

The sea had calmed down quite a bit when we turned into a westerly direction from the south, passing the dwarven capital of Dewarg and then rounding the Ferrum Mons into the Strait of Avilyn.

"What's the next step?" I asked Kennis as the lights of Avilyn Harbor were finally within our sights.

"I have been debating something," the old man began, "should I bring you all with me, or bring them all to you?"

"What are you talking about?" Meeka asked with a raised eyebrow.

"Brendt and the fairies," I guessed.

"Precisely!" The old man exclaimed, with a twinge of pride in his voice.

"Do you know where to find Brendt and the fairies?" Brother Fost asked with a suspicious tone in his own voice.

"Just as well as you do, my halfling friend," Kennis laughed and winked at the priest.

Brother Fost smiled and winked back, "I'll lead the way."

"Such a gracious offer!" Kennis teased.

The Scorpion began to turn toward the Harbor and Kennis requested that I tell the captain to instruct the helmsman to pass by and head toward the castle via the river.

The crew complied and we continued into the night toward the river.

Memories of the Water Elemental began to flood my head...

We destroyed that creature and though it may have been the only one of its kind, we didn't know, but it was either kill or be killed and our own self-preservation outweighed any thoughts of possibly sending such a race of creature into extinction.

We did what we had to do.

I must have lost track of time within my memories of that encounter, because when I finally looked around, we had already turned south again, into the river and began heading toward the exact place where the creature finally fell, once and for all.

Taking a quick look around, I witnessed both Kuchoff and Brother Fost peering over the side of the ship into the water where the battle's finale took place.

It was too dark to see.

"It will be daylight soon," Loher's voice suddenly announced from behind me.

Surprised at the sudden sound, I spun around quickly and bared my fangs.

She stood her ground: No fear.

I closed my mouth, lowered my head and backed away, "Sorry," I whispered, ashamed.

She reached out and took my hands, "It was my fault," she said, "I should have made a noise before I spoke; I am the one who should be sorry."

I smiled, making sure my fangs did not appear.

She smiled back and began to lead my back down to my box.

"I haven't fed yet," I informed.

She frowned, "Can you make do with your rats?" She asked with an uneasy shiver.

It wouldn't be the first time I had to do that, so I nodded my head and followed her down the steps, scooping up a rat on the way and drained it of its blood.

A dozen or so rats later, I stretched out in my box and drifted off, once again, into a lifeless sleep.

It wasn't quite dark yet when I awoke to the sound of a light tapping on the top of my box.

Curious, I peeked through a split I had made between two boards and saw Kennis, Kuchoff and Loher standing about three feet away and looking at whatever it was on top of my crate, making that noise.

"Can I help you?" I asked through the boards, still half asleep, but trying not to sound annoyed at the fact that I had been woken up.

"You have some special visitors," Loher announced.

"Can they wait until dark?" I asked, still dozing, now, not trying to mask my annoyance.

"No," an unknown, yet vaguely familiar female voice sternly answered back.

Her voice seemed as if it were right there in the box with me.

I peeked from a different angle through the slit, this time so I could see the top of the box and recognized the sprite, Brendt and the Queen of the fairies staring down back at me.

Brendt exaggerated a smile and wiggled his fingers in a wave.

Now wide awake and excited, I smiled without trying to hide my fangs and quickly rolled out of my box.

I stood up and rubbed my eyes; daylight was trickling in from several cracks in the decking above me.

My eyes adjusted and I noticed that there were fairies everywhere.

Several of the fairies scattered into hiding as someone came bounding down the steps.

I turned to look to see who it was as Byron, wide eyed and full of wonder in his eyes, darkened the hatch leading up.

"Fairies!" He exclaimed, "I have never seen a real fairie before! I always thought that they were a myth!"

He calmed down when he saw the serious looks on every face in the room.

"Pardon me," he exhaled noisily and turned to go back up the steps.

Before he could get very far, a dozen or so fairies blocked his path and then literally pushed him back into our group.

"Stay," the fairie Queen commanded.

"What is this all about?" The veteran soldier asked with a slight laugh, still quite astonished and wide-eyed.

"We don't have much time," the Queen announced, looking directly at me, "I must return to the Shire before nightfall.

I nodded, "What..." I began, but she cut me off.

"We are here to transport you and two escorts of your choosing, back to the future realm of the Circle of Flowers coven," she proclaimed, "choose wisely."

Loher stepped forward, "I'm going with you," she demanded, "you can't stop me."

"Of course, my love," I agreed.

"Choose one more," the Queen insisted.

"Kennis," I chose without a moment's hesitation.

"Kennis is already going," the Queen exacted, "as a continuance of the punishment I bestowed upon him long ago. You must choose again."

Kennis hung his head as if he was truly shamed, but I knew better.

I already knew that the old man wanted to return to the future realm so he could be with his daughter once again.

He was old and only getting older and he had no real place or need to be here in Beornan Heafod any longer.

I looked around at those around me and noticed that Byron had a look beyond that of excitement and wonder, while Kuchoff and Meeka looked as if they had no interest at all, "Byron, I choose Byron."

A wide smile perched upon the veteran soldier's lips.

He bowed low as if to say, 'Thank you.'

Brendt flew to Loher and landed on her shoulder.

"Then," The Queen of the fairies announced as the large group of fairies began to circle the five of us, "you shall be off!"

They all began to chant and sing, flying faster and faster until all I could see was a blur...

...My head began to swim and I became dizzy...

I felt...

...light on...

...my...

...feet...

The spinning circle of flying fairies looked as though it had become a solid ring of silver and gold, changing colors back and forth until...

Chapter Ten

FUTURI REGNI

Once again, we found ourselves near a lake, which I finally recognized as Loc Wepon, only we were now on the western side of it, while the Seolfer Wudu is on the eastern side.

It was dark, but I could see that this was the same place we had been just days before, only in our realm and in our time.

In this realm and in this time, the Charon Swamp had been filled in somehow and houses were built there now.

The tower was nowhere to be seen, which was probably a good thing, although, I had to wonder what happened to it.

I peered across the lake to see what was left of the Seolfer Wudu and breathed a sigh of relief when I saw that the forest was still there, in parts, but my home was still there.

Loher, as if reading my mind, placed her hand on my shoulder and guided me back to the house that we now knew was Shannon's.

Kennis strolled up to the door and pressed a sort of button near its side.

A bell chimed from somewhere within the house.

A moment later, one of those strange glass globes suddenly ignited, casting a soft yellowish glow around the entrance to the house and the door opened to reveal Shannon, standing in the doorway.

Her eyes went wide when she saw us standing there.

She opened the door and quickly ushered us in, looking around the area as if she was afraid that someone had seen us.

"Hello, Shannon," Kennis greeted.

Shannon stopped and stared at the old man, not realizing who he was at first, and then, it hit her, "Dad?" She asked with both alarm and joy in her voice.

"The same," Kennis laughed and held his arms out wide.

Shannon began to weep and threw herself at him, embracing him tightly, sobbing.

I wasn't sure if it was out of joy or sadness or a bit of both.

As they embraced, they mumbled things to each other that I couldn't understand.

I'm sure I wasn't supposed to.

After the embrace, the two of them stood and just looked at each other for what seemed like an hour.

Their emotions ran the whole circle, from happiness to sadness and anger and then back again until Kennis turned his daughter's attention to me, "Shannon, I'm sure you remember McLaaud and his companions," he began and then corrected himself, "well, you won't remember Byron here, he's new to the group."

Shannon looked Loher and myself over and nodded her head.

Then she realized that I had become a vampire and her eyes almost projected from her skull.

"It happened!" She cried, "Just like in my vision, you were turned Undead!"

I hung my head.

She grabbed my hand and began to pull me toward the stairs to the basement where the altar was, "We have to change you back!"

Kennis, Loher and Byron, along with a hidden Brendt followed us, close behind.

When we reached the bottom of the stairs, Shannon let go of my hand and ushered us into the altar room.

She proceeded to pull a strange object from a pocket within her clothing and tapped on it a few times and then pressed it to her ear...

"Jason?" She asked, "Yeah, it's Shannon... Call the gang and every-one get over here pronto!... I'll explain when you get here, just **move. Now!**"

She tapped on the object once again and then placed it back into her pocket.

"Don't worry, McLaaud," she assured, "we'll get you fixed up like new in no time."

I looked at Kennis with a confused look on my face.

Kennis just laughed, "You'll be fine, my boy, just fine," he said, "take a seat and rest a while, my daughter's friends will be here soon and we can then get started."

The old man looked at his daughter with a longing look in his eyes.

Shannon was staring at me with a thoughtful look in her own.

It was as if she was used to seeing vampires and elves on a daily basis but I knew that it was really because she had grown up with the understanding that other Realms really do exist and they house creatures far different than her own.

Or, perhaps she had indeed seen an actual vampire before.

She was, in fact, the one that was supposed to be able to bring me back to the world of the living.

One would hope that she had done this before.

A moment later, there was a loud knock on the door that we had used to enter the house and then the sounds of several sets of footsteps above us.

The footsteps wandered to the stairs leading to the basement and began to descend toward us.

"Relax, it's just Jason and the rest of the coven," Shannon softly announced. "Surely you remember Jason."

I nodded my head.

"Your boyfriend?" Kennis half laughed.

Shannon began to blush a bit, "Well, no, not exactly," she stated, "I wouldn't mind though."

Just then, as if on cue, Jason and about eight or ten other people, some of which I vaguely remembered, came through the door and lined up against the far wall.

Almost every eye was on me, some gazes, at times, would dart around the room and seek out Kennis, Loher and Byron, but they all eventually returned to me.

A large black cat, the size of a cocker spaniel, wandered into the room and hopped nonchalantly into Loher's lap; this, the she-elf seemed to like and accepted it as a sign of good things to come.

After a few moments of everyone shuffling around and finding suitable spots to settle, Shannon stood at the end of the altar and raised her hands in the air to gain the attention of all present.

"I have gathered you all here tonight because my clairvoyant vision of the vampire came true as you all can obviously see," she announced and motioned toward me.

Now, everyone turned and looked directly at me as I playfully flashed my fangs and smiled for effect.

Gasps of horror and awe filled the room.

One human male uttered the word, 'cool,' although I'm not quite sure what the temperature of the room had to do with anything.

"McLaaud here," she continued, "I'm sure you all remember him, has become a vampire, as my vision predicted. He has returned here, seeking our help in restoring his life force."

There was an excited buzz about the room.

The word 'cool' was again uttered several times, but still, I felt no obvious change in the temperature of the room.

Shannon smiled and continued, "I am pleased to see that none of you are afraid of Mr. McLaaud. He **is** here by his own choice and is not interested in harming any of us."

The excited buzz grew stronger and Shannon had to purposely clear her throat in order to regain everyone's attention.

"Now," she continued, "you all know what your assigned duties are in this situation, so if you will all perform them to the best of your abilities, we can succeed in our task and send our friends back as soon as possible."

Upon completion of this statement, the witches began to gather in small groups around the room.

Some were lighting candles while others lit sweet smelling incense, while others still, began to softly chant in small circles about the room.

When the candles were lit and the incense was burning, the witches gathered into a group as a whole and continued to chant.

I have to admit that I found this all extremely enchanting and exciting.

Shannon and Jason walked up to my companions and me.

Jason put his hand on Byron's shoulder, "It's fortunate that you came along, my friend," he told the veteran soldier, "McLaaud is half human and he will need a strong human to help him recover."

Byron looked confused, "Recover?" He asked.

Jason smiled, "He will need a small portion of your human life force transfused into him."

"He will need a portion of your elven life force as well," Shannon explained to Loher.

"I'm willing to do whatever it takes to return him to normal," Loher committed.

"How do we..." Byron paused, thinking, "donate... some life force to him?" He asked.

Shannon and Jason lead Loher, Byron and me to the door that lead to where the air tight chamber was located.

⚬

Upon opening the door, a large room was revealed.

Within this large room, I saw the airtight chamber, that I assumed I would be placed into, as well as a half dozen rack like contraptions with restraints, and a few cot-like beds.

In the center of the room there was a box-like contraption that was tethered to the wall, quite like the flameless torches with glass bulbs; I think the fairies called them 'lamps.'

The tether on the boxlike thing was a lot thicker and black as opposed to the thin tethers of the lamps.

There were two other tether-like cords extending from the box, one black, one red.

Each had a long metal rod at the end; an odd looking thing.

"What **is** that thing?" I asked, and motioned to the box.

"That is an industrial battery charger that we modified to send out controlled bursts of electricity," Jason explained. "Although, I'm sure you have no idea what electricity is."

I shook my head, 'no.'

"Man-made lightning," Shannon stated.

I nodded, but still didn't fully understand.

On the far wall, there was yet another door, made of steel and brandishing a very large and very sturdy looking bolt type lock.

"What's in there?" I asked, pointing to the locked steel door.

"Contained within that room is the reason we are able to return the life force to a willing vampire," Shannon proudly answered.

"It also helps us rid the world of annoying pests," Jason laughed but then fell quiet as Shannon shot him a look that would have killed him if looks could indeed kill.

Shannon regained her composure, "We are going to need you, McLaaud, to step into the glass chamber and the two of you, if you would lie down on these racks and allow us to strap you in, we will be under way."

"What are you going to do to us?" Byron asked, a bit of nervousness in his voice.

(and rightfully so!)

Shannon chuckled, "Oh! Where are my manners?" She laughed, "That room contains a creature, that will begin to extract the life force from each of you, but we won't let it take too much or you'll obviously die."

"How will you stop it?" Loher calmly asked.

"We have it secured to a movable rack like the one I'm strapping you into right now," She explained as she tightened the restraints around Loher's wrists. "When the creature has extracted enough life force from each of you, we will move it into the chamber with McLaaud and shock it with our modified battery charger." "The shock will make the creature expel the life force into the chamber around the vampire **and** knock the creature out, temporarily," Jason continued, "the vampire will then have to turn into a vaporous mist and absorb the life force, which will solidify the then **ex**-vampire/now living person while we wheel the creature back to the room, lock the door and the ex-vampire, and willing life force donators rest until fully recovered."

"That's it?" I asked.

"That's it," Shannon confirmed.

"You have done this before?" I asked.

"You will be our third case in less than ten years," Shannon assured.

"Seems easy enough," Byron admitted, now strapped to his rack.

"Believe me," Jason sighed, "it's more complicated than it sounds."

"How do you keep the creature from sucking **your** life force?" Loher asked, also strapped to her rack.

⸺◆⸺

"We have special... armor... that we wear," Shannon answered and showed us an odd looking flexible one-piece suit with an attached domed helmet and glasslike face shield.

"These are made of a material called rubber," Shannon continued, "after we put these on, the creature cannot suck out our life force and we are able to move it around with no harm done to ourselves."

"Is rubber stronger than iron or steel?" Byron asked.

"In some ways it is, I guess," Shannon chuckled, "but in most conventional ways, no, it's not."

"Rubber will not stop an arrow or a blade unless it is extremely thick," Jason added, "the thicker rubber is, the less it bends. The less rubber bends, the less we are able to move around in it and that becomes a problem."

"If you wouldn't mind stepping into the chamber now, McLaaud," Shannon said with a sweeping motion of her hand toward the chamber, "we will put our suits on and get started."

I took a quick glance at Loher and then walked over and stepped into the chamber.

Jason and Shannon put the odd rubber suits on and then unlocked and opened the large steel door.

They disappeared inside for a moment and then emerged, rolling out a rack on wheels with a creature identified as a Vita Comedénti, thought to be extinct, even in my time, strapped securely to it.

Vita Comedénti are so powerful psychically, that they appear to their victims as extremely attractive.

Once the victim is influenced by the psychic bond, it is virtually impossible to break the attraction, hence, the restraints on the racks.

As long as Shannon or Jason refrains from looking into its eyes, they will not be drawn to the creature.

I noticed that as they wheeled it out of the room, they both stayed behind it.

They also took the precaution of putting a strip of cloth or some other type of material over its eyes.

"Will it still be able to drain our life force without us being attracted to it?" Byron asked.

"The attraction only helps prevent its victim's escape," Jason explained, "quite like the sticky stuff on a fly trap plant."

Confused, Byron just smiled, shook his head and closed his eyes in an attempt to relax.

At first, it didn't seem like anything was happening to Loher and Byron, but after a few moments of exposure, they began to turn ghastly pale and physically weak as their heads began to drop and loll a bit.

With the rubber suits on, I couldn't identify who had the rolling cart, but whoever it was began to quickly roll the Vita Comedénti toward the chamber as the other unstrapped Loher and Byron and guided them each to a cot.

With the donors now safely tucked into bed and the Vita Comedénti positioned at the chamber door, the witch that unstrapped my companions quickly rushed over and flipped a switch on the lightning box, grabbed the red and black cords and then swiftly moved close to the chamber door.

The witches, together, counted down from three and then shocked the Vita Comedénti.

Before the sparks from the shocking were even on the floor, they had the creature out and the door shut and sealed with a loud hiss.

I had never turned into a vaporous mist before and I wasn't exactly sure how to do it, so I gave it my best shot.

The next thing I knew, I was waking up in a cot next to Loher.

She was breathing and fast asleep.

The color had returned to her skin and she looked peaceful... Beautiful.

Byron was fast asleep in the cot next to her, his color had returned and he looked peaceful as well.

We were alone in the room and the big steel door was closed and bolted locked.

I ran my tongue across my teeth and felt no fangs.

My hands looked almost as they did before that damn messenger showed up at my door, only a bit more calloused and rough.

I was hungry.

Hunger.

A real hunger like I hadn't felt for what seemed like eternity.

Not for blood but for food.

Real food.

I tried to get off of the cot, but my body was just too weak.

The beating of my heart in my chest was apparent and soothing and its rhythm had me soon fast asleep again.

When I awoke once again, Loher was standing next to me.

Byron was there as well as Kennis and Shannon.

"How do you feel, my love?" Loher asked, a huge smile had invaded her face.

"Alive," I answered and Loher began to laugh, "and **hungry!**" I completed.

"There is a feast waiting for you in the kitchen," Shannon commented.

"Let us go eat," Byron coughed.

"We waited for you," Loher added, still smiling.

She helped me off the cot and guided me through the basement and up the stairs.

Through the window, I could see the glorious sun shining brightly in the sky.

There were quite a lot of clouds, but there was the sun, beautiful against the bright, robin's egg blue sky.

We entered the kitchen and the fragrance of real food invaded my nostrils and tempted my stomach which was singing out loud enough for the others to hear.

I didn't care what it was that I was eating; some sort of long white stringy things smothered in a reddish sauce filled with tiny bits of beef and tomatoes along with green peppers, onions and mushrooms.

It had a funny name that I had never heard before, something like pasketty.

Whatever it was, it was delicious and I ate a lot of it.

When I was done, I felt as if my belly would burst, but then Shannon brought out some chocolate chip cookies and my thoughts settled on Kuchoff.

Shannon served cow's milk in clear glass mugs without handles; it tasted weak, but it was refreshing and went well with the cookies.

————◦————

It was time for us to return to our own realm.

"If there is ever anything we can do to repay you..." Loher began to offer, but Shannon cut her off...

"My father explained to me that Corrina, the dark witch that went with him to the other realm, was killed by falling from a window at the top of the tower," she began, "I want you to somehow destroy that tower, that will repay us."

"Consider it done," Byron pledged.

Loher and I agreed, "Balt will enjoy that task," I said with a smile, excited to get back to Beornan Heafod and rejoin the rest of my friends.

"The dwarf, right?" Shannon asked.

"Yes," I confirmed, "you have a very good memory."

"He stuck out in my mind because he was very protective of you and your companions," Shannon conveyed, "Now where is Brendt?"

"I don't know," I laughed, remembering that the sprite had come with us.

There was suddenly a bright flash, "You called?" Brendt sang as he appeared from the flash.

"Where have you been?" Shannon asked in a giggle, "No, on second thought, don't answer that, I don't want to know, just send them back to their own realm please."

"Where in the realm would you like to go?" The sprite asked.

My companions and I looked at each other for a moment and then without discussion, we visually agreed, "The Scorpion," I answered.

"As you wish," Brendt laughed.

As I had learned to expect, the room began to spin and I felt my body go limp and light on my feet.

The basement was no longer surrounding us, but instead, I was wet and slightly cold as I found myself on the wooden deck, rocking motion and all; heavy rain pouring down on my head.

The Scorpion!

EPILOGUE

Land was nowhere in sight and it was raining so hard that we could barely see each other when we appeared back on the deck of The Scorpion.

"Where are we?" I asked, having to yell loudly over the sound of the torrential storm beating on the ship.

"I have no idea!" Byron yelled back, "I'm not a sailor; I'm a land loving soldier!"

"We have to find Captain Waxx!" I hollered back.

"Below decks!" Loher called and grabbed my hand.

We ran through the rain, barely able to see where we were going, but could see well enough to notice that there was no one else in sight.

"Where is the crew?" I asked whoever could hear me.

"What?" Byron called from behind.

"I said," I slowed and let him catch up, "where is the crew? There's no one on deck!"

"That's what I thought you said!" Byron yelled over the rain.

"Come on!" Loher yelled, "Let's get below!"

My stomach hurt, not only from eating too much of Shannon's pasketty, but now from the gripping thought that we had been 'blinked' to a derelict ship drifting far off into nowhere.

This **was** The Scorpion, no other ship that I've seen looked like a giant floating golden statue of a scorpion; she was a one-of-a-kind.

As we ran to the steps that led to the ship's belly, we could see a light coming from down below.

I tugged on Loher's arm and made her stop.

I leaned up close to her ear and said, "Let me go first, there might be trouble!"

Loher agreed and motioned Byron to stand by.

The veteran soldier complied.

I remembered that I had procured a cloak of shadows from the tower, so I slipped the hood over my head and vanished.

Invisible, I slowly slipped my way carefully down the steps and peeked around the corner into the hold.

Everyone was down there, the captain, the entire crew and our companions, accompanied by a large group of orc marauders and a single, elderly human male.

The human was dressed in purple robes of the magic sort and I assumed that he was in control of the orc marauders.

Balt looked beat up quite badly, but Brother Fost was tending to his wounds.

Meeka was bound with ties and gagged, while Kuchoff was lying on the floor, not moving; I couldn't tell if he was alive or dead.

They must have taken the crew by surprise because I didn't see any dead orcs anywhere; the storm must have been their cover.

Then, the thought occurred to me, perhaps this was an un-natural storm, created by the robe clad human...

I snuck back up the steps.

"We need that new bow of yours," I whispered in Loher's ear while holding a hand up to Byron, letting him know to be patient.

The three of us huddled together as I explained the situation in detail and we came up with a plan.

Loher strung up her new bow as Byron and I readied our blades.

On the silent count of three, Loher cloaked herself and then led the way down the steps and fired multiple arrows at the purple robed human, taking the whole party, our companions included, by complete surprise.

As Loher's arrows found purchase in the body of the robed one, our blades found their marks as well, as one by one, the orcs fell.

Balt took this chance to grab a fallen sword and join in the fight until he could get his ruddy little hands on his beloved Great Axe.

Brother Fost rushed over and cut Meeka free and then attended to the apparently still living Kuchoff.

The sounds of angry battle raged on below decks as sailors took up arms and grievously joined the cause.

We made quick work of the enemy as they were outnumbered almost three to one.

"Dem sharks be eatin' good tonight, Bruddah!" Captain Waxx cheered as we met among the corpses of the fallen.

After a moment's pause to catch our breath and survey the damage, my curiosity got the best of me, "What happened, Captain?" I asked.

"De storm juss came outta nowhere, Mon," the captain began, "an' dey juss appeared outta nowhere too, juss like you and yor friends do."

"No ship?" I asked.

The captain's eyes went wide when he finally took a good look at me, and then a big smile sprang out upon his lips, "Yor not a vampire no-more!" He realized.

The storm had slowed down to a steady rain and continued to weaken to an eventual stop as the wind had all but died away.

The glorious sun began to peek out from behind the clouds, burning them away and delivering a nice, clear, calm day.

"No ship?" I repeated and returned a finally fangless smile.

"No, Mon," the captain answered, "no ship, juss a big lightning crack an' a puff of brown smoke an' den dare dey were."

"Obvious magic of some sort," I mentioned.

"Perhaps yor sexy wizard lady friend can tell us what it was, Bruddah," Captain Waxx chuckled, relieved that there was no lasting damage to his ship or crew.

We ventured up the steps and surveyed the surrounding area to see where we were.

The decks were rain soaked, but the crewmen were well on their way drying it up the best that they could.

"Do you know where we are?" I asked the captain as he checked with his telescope and sextant.

"No," he answered, his lips now vacant of a trace of a smile, "not a clue, Mon."

My now beating heart sank a bit.

The captain nodded and hurriedly walked away to talk to a few of his trusted crewmen about rectifying the situation.

I stood there for a moment or two to collect my thoughts and stare out to sea in hopes that I would see land at best, or perhaps another ship.

My companions were searching the bodies of the dead orc marauders or helping The Scorpion's crew clean up the mess.

The corpses were searched, stripped of anything useful and then tossed, one by one overboard.

I began to stroll about the ship and survey the situation and as I did, I passed by members of the crew that looked pleased and relieved as they saw me, that I was no longer Undead.

I decided to seek out my companions.

The first of my companions that I found were Byron, Brother Fost and Kuchoff.

"How is he?" I asked after coaxing the priest away from the boy.

"He'll live," the halfling answered, "he is a very brave young man. As soon as one of the orcs grabbed Meeka, he attacked. Unfortunately, he did minor damage to her assailant and was thrashed within a thread of his life and left for dead." The priest looked at me, "Another question is, how are *you* doing now that you're 'alive' again?" He asked with a relieved smile and concern in his eyes.

"I'll live," I answered with a wink and smile at my echoed reply and motioned him back to his patient, "I'll check on you in a bit."

"We will be here," Fost said and turned back to Kuchoff, "he's not going anywhere for a while."

I walked away, not knowing what to do or how to feel now; I decided to catch up with Balt.

I found him and Loher searching the remainder of the orc corpses before some crew members took them away to be shark food.

Meeka was leaning over the dead human, reading a small book she had found in his robes; she wouldn't let anyone near him until she was sure she had everything the corpse had to offer.

Loher's arrows still protruded from his chest along with one expertly placed arrow directly in the center of his forehead.

I walked over and tried to yank the arrow from his forehead.

It took some effort and some wiggling but I got it out with no damage to the arrow head.

Blood and grey brain matter dripped from the sharpened tip and made a slight splattering sound when it made contact with the floor.

I inspected the projectile and was amazed at the nearly perfect condition it was still in.

"Here, Loher," I said as I offered the arrow back to her, "A souvenir."

She took the arrow, looked at it, shrugged her shoulders and smiled and then put the arrow back into her quiver, "Thanks," she said and returned to the corpse she was searching.

"Oi, Mate!" Balt exclaimed.

I turned and looked at the dwarf.

"Ye be **alive**!" He testified.

I just smiled as the dwarf stood and looked at me.

"Bout time," he grunted and went back to the sword he was inspecting.

"Meeka," I softly called to get her attention, but not to disturb her too much as she was probably deeply consumed in whatever magic book she was reading.

After a short pause, the wizard looked up and lightly shook the cobwebs out of her mind, returning to our version of reality.

She smiled as she realized that I was no longer a vampire, "How is Kuchoff?"

"Brother Fost says that he'll live and be good as new in no time," I half lied.

"That orc trounced him pretty badly and there was nothing anyone could do to stop it," she reported and looked back down at the cover of the book she held.

"Do you have any idea who that man was?" I asked, trying not to sound too interested.

She looked down at the corpse in front of her and frowned, "No," she shook her head, "but these robes look familiar, I'm sure I have seen them before. I think they belong to some sort of religious order or cult or something, but who, I couldn't begin to say."

This answer shocked me and made chills run up my spine.

"So this wasn't some sort of random attack," I rhetorically commented.

"No," she agreed, "This had purpose behind it, but who was he and what did he want?"

"I believe the proper term to use would be 'they' not 'he,' Meeka," I added, "if he belonged to some sort of order, or sect, or cult or something, he did not act alone and I think we may not have seen the last of them."

"Like I said before," she reminded, "I can't be sure of where or what he came from." The wizard lowered her eyes and opened the book again, to the page she was studying, and continued to read.

I watched my companions delve into their chosen duties for a while and then decided to return to the bridge to see if the captain had any luck finding out where we were.

When I surfaced back to the deck, I saw that the crew had everything back in proper order as if the skirmish had never taken place; all but the crew members that were still hauling orc corpses to the railing and dumping them overboard.

Curiously, I looked behind the ship and saw a trail of bodies in our wake; I had to laugh.

When I arrived at the bridge, Captain Waxx and his helmsman were leaning over a spread out map and had very confused looks on their faces.

"Any luck finding out where we are?" I innocently asked.

The captain and helmsman looked up and Captain Waxx shook his head, "Not a clue, Mon, I 'ave been ev'ry where on dees wat'rs an' know my way to ev'ry Port, but we cannot find our bearings no matter 'ow much we be lookin'."

"So, we're lost," I muttered.

"Correct, Mon, an' it gets worse," he warned and pointed to the horizon.

I looked out, over the sea and all I saw were dark clouds surrounding us as if we were in the eye of a great storm, only this storm was closing in on us.

That pain in my stomach went from a dull throb from too much food to a sharp stab of anxiety, fear and worry in an instant.

The captain and helmsman went back to looking at the map and my thoughts went to my companions below deck.

I had to warn them.

"How long?" I asked.

"We be battenin' down de hatches in less dan an hour, Mon," the captain half groaned, "Dis is gonna be a bad one."

<The End>

If you enjoyed **Dark** please post a review
and enjoy Thunor and his party's continuing adventures in
Vast: Book Three of The Scorpion Chronicles.

www.ingramcontent.com/pod-product-compliance
Lightning Source LLC
Chambersburg PA
CBHW021200310726
48971CB00002B/722